THUNDER OVER TABOR

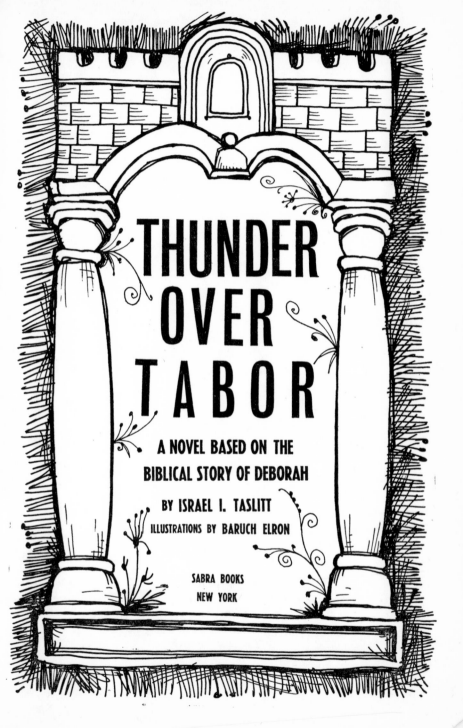

THUNDER OVER TABOR

A NOVEL BASED ON THE BIBLICAL STORY OF DEBORAH

BY ISRAEL I. TASLITT

ILLUSTRATIONS BY BARUCH ELRON

SABRA BOOKS
NEW YORK

SBN 87631—022—6
Library of Congress Catalog Card Number 75—103111
Printed in Israel by Ben-Nun Press, Tel Aviv

CONTENTS

BY WAY OF INTRODUCTION

O f the twelve tribes of Israel who were to inherit the Promised Land, nine and one-half were settled by Joshua in Canaan, west of the Jordan River, in the territory "from Dan to Beersheba," from Phoenicia in the north to the land of the Philistines in the south.

The Canaanites tried to check the advancing Israelites but were defeated. They had to accept the presence of the Israelite settlers, whose God they feared because of all the miracles He had wrought for the Children of Israel, beginning with their exodus from Egyptian bondage.

Things changed when Joshua died. Left without a leader, the Israelites felt that they would be safe only if they gained the friendship of their neighbors — even if it meant turning their backs on their own God and worshipping Canaanite gods.

But the Canaanites — and the Amorites, Moabites and other peoples among whom the Israelites now lived — thought otherwise. If the Israelites wanted to

7

worship other gods, they reasoned, it was surely because their God had abandoned them. No people in its right mind would turn away, of its own will, from such a powerful God!

The enemies of the Israelites therefore took heart. First the Moabites and then the Philistines fell upon the Israelite tribes and enslaved them.

Several generations after the Israelites first entered Canaan, the Canaanites in the far north, above the Sea of Galilee, also became powerful enough to enslave the Israelites who lived among them.

How they became powerful, how the Israelites fought back, and how an historic woman led the Israelite revolt, will be found in the pages of *Thunder Over Tabor*.

I.I.T.

CHAPTER ONE

THE CLASH ON THE HIGHWAY

A mule-drawn cart was rattling south along the rocky highway from Bethel to Ramah. On either side, the ridges of the Mount Ephraim range rose and dipped against the blue morning sky.

In the driver's seat was a boy of about sixteen. He wore the plain loose garments of the Galileans, and on his head perched a rough straw hat which suggested that he was its designer as well. His hands on the reins were firm and sure, and to pass the time he kept up a one-sided conversation with the grayish-black mule trotting ahead of him.

In the cart, behind the boy, an old man lay asleep on a matting of hay. The rattling of the wheels on the stony road did not disturb him until the cart bounced off a stone that had rolled down the hillside. Then, awaking with a start, he blinked up at the sun, and drew himself up to the seat beside the boy.

"Halt, O Pered, son of the wind," the youth called out merrily to the mule. "See you not that my grandfather is awake? It is time for the morning meal, as

I am sure you well know." He guided the mule to the side of the road and jumped down to the ground.

The old man shook his hair and beard clear of the hay. "Are we almost there, Arnon?" he asked. "Perhaps you have strayed off the road?"

"We shall be there very soon, Grandfather," the boy replied, "for we are beyond Bethel. Besides, you know very well that Pered never takes any more steps than he has to and he would have to be a mountain goat to wander off anywhere in these hills."

The old man waved his wrinkled hand impatiently. "Do not find fault with the mule," he said. "I am sure that you can talk him into all kinds of pranks." Again he looked up at the sun. "We should have stopped earlier," he exclaimed. "Let us therefore have our meal lest it be said that Avinoam starves his grandson."

While Arnon unharnessed Pered, Avinoam dug into the hay at the foot of the cart and brought forth a pitcher and a small sack. From the sack he fished out a wedge of goat's cheese, salted olives wrapped in vine leaves, and a loaf of brown-crusted bread. All these he set out on a low flat boulder by the side of the highway.

"Yes, it is good that we eat now," Avinoam observed, as he and his grandson propped themselves against the rock. "Once we get to Ramah, you will no doubt be running off in all directions at once."

Arnon, in the middle of a generous mouthful, shook his head. "I shall be most well behaved, Grandfather," he finally managed to say. "You'll see. People will stop one another and ask: 'Who is this quiet, dignified

young man?' And they will be told: 'It is Arnon, of Kedesh that is in the territory of Naftali; the son of Barak and the grandson of Avinoam.' Will this not make you proud, O Grandfather?"

Avinoam looked at his grandson in mock disgust. "It is clear that you are a victim of the sun," he said. "I shall be satisfied if we are not ordered to leave the Spring Market because of your antics."

Arnon bent forward to see what Pered was doing. The mule was munching away at his fodder, but he did not look any happier than when he was drawing the cart. The boy leaned back and reached for the cheese. "Tell me, Grandfather," he said, "is the Spring Market of Ramah really as exciting as I have heard it said?"

The old man eyed his grandson sternly. "Excitement... adventure... mischief! That is all you care about, isn't it?" He shook a bony finger at the boy. "I insist that you spend some time listening to the wise words of the Prophetess Deborah. You will learn more from her in a brief hour than you will from the haggling of the merchants in three days."

"As you say, Grandfather," replied Arnon cheerfully. "You may not think so, but I am truly eager to see the Prophetess and to hear her judge the people. To think that a woman should be so wise!"

Avinoam threw up his hands in horror. "So now you are doubting the wisdom of women!" he scoffed. "If my worthy daughter-in-law, your mother, were to hear you, this would be your last trip to the Spring Market as well as your first!"

12

Arnon did not seem to be alarmed. "I speak in jest, Grandfather. Deborah must indeed be wise if people come from all over the land to seek her advice and abide by her judgment."

The old man grunted but said nothing. Arnon was a fine lad, though he appeared interested in little except swimming and running races and wrestling with the shepherd boys.

The two had almost finished their meal when Arnon caught sight of a figure clambering down the slope on the other side of the road. The newcomer leaped nimbly from one boulder to the next, then alighted on the hard-packed earth and advanced toward the cart, his arm raised in a friendly greeting.

"Peace be with you," he cried. "Can you spare a gulp of water for a thirsty wanderer ?"

"In peace be your coming," Avinoam replied. He held out the pitcher. "Drink until you are refreshed."

The stranger lifted the jug above his upturned face and let the cool water gurgle down his throat.

"You are welcome to partake of cheese and olives," offered Arnon.

"Many thanks, from the heart," the stranger said. "Kindness, along with food, is a princely blessing for Benjamin the Wanderer." He sat down beside the boulder and helped himself to a piece of cheese, then he turned to Avinoam. "Your blessing, sir."

Avinoam closed his eyes. "Though I am not of the tribe of Levi, I give you my blessing willingly. In your wanderings, O Benjamin, may you lack for neither food nor water, and may the blessings of peace always attend you on your way."

Arnon watched the man who called himself Benjamin the Wanderer as he bit into the cheese. Despite his ragged and dusty garments he did not look like a beggar. He had a rather wide face and a black beard.

"To judge from the cheese," Benjamin said, "you must come from the north. It is excellent to the taste."

"Indeed that is where we come from," Arnon replied. "From Kedesh, in the territory of Naftali."

Benjamin slapped his thigh. "Ha, Kedesh! A fine place. A most delightful town. Many a time have I passed through it in the course of my wanderings." He took another sip from the pitcher. "You are no doubt bound for the Spring Market at Ramah?"

"Indeed we are," Arnon replied grandly. "My first visit there!"

Benjamin leaned back on his elbow. "You will be delighted with the Market," he observed. "Few towns in this territory can boast of such a fine gathering. Merchants, caravans..."

"Few towns, yes," Avinoam interrupted. For the first time there was a ring in his voice. "And who knows how long the market at Ramah will go on. Each year our merchants are growing poorer."

"I understand it very well, sir," Benjamin commented soberly. "King Jabin of Hazor has the tribes of Israel in his power."

Avinoam nodded sadly. "King Jabin and Commander Sisera, with his nine hundred iron chariots. From the waters of Merom to Mount Tabor these chariots shake the peace of Israel." The old man sigh-

14

ed. "Yes, we are in the hands of Jabin and Sisera even as our fathers were in the power of King Eglon and the Moabites."

"But didn't Ehud, the son of Gera, break the Moabite yoke?" Arnon broke in, spiritedly. "We must find a way to do the same, else every tribe in Israel will find itself enslaved."

Avinoam reached out and placed his hand on his grandson's knee, as a sign of warning. This Benjamin did not look or speak like a Canaanite, but it was said that King Jabin had spies everywhere. "Oppression is not easy to bear," the old man said slowly, "yet we must live with it until better days come." He paused for a moment. "You say you have been in Kedesh. Do you know anyone there?"

"Do you know my father, Barak the wool merchant?" Arnon asked eagerly.

A sudden twinkle came into the stranger's eye. "The wool merchant?" he repeated. "Yes, I believe I have heard of him. A fine man."

Avinoam began gathering up the cheese, bread and olives that were left. "Let us be on our way," he urged. "We set out from Kedesh at dawn so that we might reach Ramah in time to hear the Prophetess," he explained to Benjamin. "Usually she holds court not far from here. But her home is in Ramah."

Arnon, meanwhile, had talked Pered into going back to his task. He was about to back the mule between the shafts of the cart when the rumble of iron wheels came from around a bend in the road and a chariot came headlong in a cloud of dust. Without slackening speed, the chariot swung out in a wide arc and swept across the road straight at the wooden cart.

"Beware!" cried Arnon, yanking Pered off to one side, while Benjamin pulled Avinoam out of the way. Through the dust, they saw the driver of the chariot tug desperately at the reins, but his speed was too great. Before he could pull the chariot out of the curve, it had crashed against the frail cart, smashing it to splinters.

The jolt threw the horses enough off stride for the driver to bring them to a halt a few paces away.

"It is one of King Jabin's royal chariots," Benjamin exclaimed in an undertone. "We had better hold our peace," he added, as he noticed the flash of anger in Arnon's eyes.

As the dust settled, the three travelers saw that there was another person in the chariot besides the burly driver. He was a tall, well-built man, with the stern features of one accustomed to command. He walked up to the demolished cart and gave it a brief glance. "You should have drawn it farther back from the road," he observed coldly.

Arnon, despite Benjamin's warning, could not restrain himself. "Had we known you were coming, sir," he exclaimed, "we would have drawn the cart up to the top of the hill."

The charioteer took a step forward, whip upraised. "You dare speak thus to Prince Etzer, you green pup?" he shouted. "One more word from you and I'll flay you alive!"

Benjamin's hand moved slowly toward his cloak as

Avinoam vainly tried to pull his grandson back. But Arnon paid no heed. "All this wouldn't have happened," he retorted, "if you'd known how to handle a chariot!"

With a cry of rage the driver lunged at Arnon, bringing his whip down at the same time, but the boy, flinging himself forward under the blow, hit the driver at the knees. The latter fell like an oak and sprawled on his back over the stony ground.

"Enough of this!" the man called Prince Etzer exclaimed, before either Arnon or the driver could get to his feet. Again he glanced at the cart. "I suggest that in the future you be on the lookout for our chariots." He turned to his bruised charioteer. "On our way, Nehag—if you are not too badly hurt."

The sarcasm in Prince Etzer's voice was not lost on the driver. He picked up his whip and got into the chariot without a word. He stood there, staring straight ahead, until his master had climbed aboard. A moment later the three were alone again.

Benjamin placed himself squarely in front of Arnon. "Young man," he said severely, "you are indeed fortunate that Prince Etzer is not as vicious as some of the other nobles of Hazor, else you might have fared very badly."

Arnon lowered his head, but there was defiance in his voice. "He called me a green pup, didn't he?"

"That he did," replied Benjamin cheerfully. "Yet a live pup, green or of any other color, has certain advantages over a dead lion."

Avinoam, breathing freely for the first time in many

minutes, nodded in quick agreement. "Our friend is right, Arnon," he exclaimed. "Brute force belongs to the Canaanites and their chariots, and foolhardy is he who challenges their might."

Benjamin was ruefully surveying the wrecked cart. "Too bad that we are not in need of kindling wood," he remarked. "There is a month's supply right here."

Avinoam sighed. "Perhaps this is an omen," he said. "It may be best that we return to Kedesh, if this is how our visit to Ramah has begun." Then his wrinkled face lit up into a smile. "Or perhaps we are being put to the test. To see and hear the Prophetess is a privilege indeed worth the sacrifice."

Arnon's mind was on more practical things than omens and sacrifices. "It looks as though we'll have to continue on foot, Grandfather," he said. "Perhaps a merchant on his way to the Market will overtake us."

Benjamin shook his head. "Any merchant with any intention of being in Ramah for the market is already there," he observed. He turned to Avinoam. "I suggest, sir, that you ride the mule. We shall serve as your escort."

Arnon helped his grandfather to mount Pered, who did not seem to have any opinion about the change one way or the other. The three then moved away from the scene of their encounter with the Canaanites.

"You say that you are the son of Barak?" Benjamin asked Arnon.

"Yes," the boy replied. "But why do you ask?"

"No reason at all," replied Benjamin. "No reason at all." But again the twinkle came into his eyes.

CHAPTER TWO

THE FIRST MEETING

It lacked a short hour until midnight when Arnon was wakened from sleep by sharp tug at his cloak.

He roused himself with an effort. Not more than four hours had passed since he had stretched himself out, exhausted on the cot in the lodging house.

The afternoon had been long for the boy from Kedesh, long and thrilling. The three had arrived at Ramah sooner than they expected, thanks to a kind-hearted farmer who overtook them with his wagon not far past the splintered remains of the cart. The colorful stalls in the marketplace were doing a brisk business. The sing-song of the merchants, chanting the praises of their wares, rose and fell on Arnon's ears like the buzz of bewildered bees. Still the sound was far more pleasant than the shrill cries of those who, not having been blessed with melodious voices, did their best to drown out their more gifted brethren.

Toward late afternoon, Arnon noticed that the people in the market place were beginning to drift away toward the western end of Ramah. This meant, as Benjamin the Wanderer had told him earlier, that Deborah was about to open her court. Arnon hastened back to the inn to fetch Avinoam.

Famous though the Prophetess now was throughout the length and breadth of the land, no one seemed to know anything about her early years. The name of her husband was said to be Lapidoth, but none had ever laid eyes on him. Rumor had it that he had been killed by the Canaanites, for it was at the height of the oppression by Jabin that Deborah first appeared in Ramah. At first she was known simply as a wise woman who made peace between neighbors. Soon she was asked to settle disputes among the townspeople, and before long, her fame began to spread everywhere by admiring merchants returned home from the market.

Arnon found his grandfather waiting for him impatiently. Benjamin had disappeared, leaving Avinoam alone in the busy courtyard of the crowded inn.

"Are you really calling for me, or have you come here by mistake?" the old man asked sharply. "Ah better the quiet of Kedesh than the tumult of Ramah and its Spring Market, I tell you."

Arnon helped Avinoam to his feet. "The Prophetess will soon begin holding court, Grandfather," he said. "Let us hasten."

"Let us fly like the eagle," muttered Avinoam. "Fortunate shall we be if we are in time to see the Prophetess."

For once Avinoam's worry was groundless. They came to the edge of the gathering crowd, at the bot-

tom of a gentle slope, within easy sight of Deborah. She was sitting on a wide bench, listening closely to several men who were arguing their case before her. At her side, a barrel-chested man with a voice like the blast of a *shofar* (a ram's horn) repeated the arguments for everyone to hear. Then came the testimony of witnesses and, finally, Deborah's decision, which was greeted with cheers of admiration from the assemblage below.

Hours later, over their supper, the merchants went over the cases that they had heard. All agreed that not since the days of Miriam, sister of Moses and Aaron, had there been such a remarkable woman in Israel. As for Arnon, it was all he could do to remember something of what he had heard to tell his friends back in Kedesh. He was dreaming about it in his sleep when the tug at his cloak aroused him.

"Quiet!" grunted a voice in his ear. "Get up and come with me."

Arnon's eyes blinked open. In the gloom of the low chamber, he could make out the burly figure of the innkeeper.

"What do you want?" Arnon asked sleepily.

"Someone to see you," the other growled.

Arnon slid silently off the cot, gathered his cloak about him, and followed the innkeeper out into the courtyard. From inside the inn came the clatter of kitchenware.

A torch was burning in the courtyard, and in its light Arnon saw a hooded figure, standing just outside the doorway. The innkeeper disappeared. The mysterious figure moved toward the gate, beckoning him to follow. Arnon, now fully awake, made a startling discovery. Without any doubt, the figure walking ahead of him was that of a girl.

At the gate she paused. Several merchants were still lolling about, too tired after the long day for anything but scraps of idle conversation. They broke off abruptly as Arnon and his guide passed through the gate into the street.

"Hah! Young people should be in bed at this hour," one of the merchants growled. "But you can't tell the Ramah people how to run things in their town. Now in *my* town..."

"Youngsters nowadays are not what they used to be," another broke in. "Your town, my town, Ramah! Things are not the same today, and I blame the Canaanites. Now as for the price of wool this year..." His voice faded away into the cool night air.

Arnon was tempted to halt the girl and ask her a few questions, but she kept ahead of him, walking briskly through the deserted market place. Soon they were heading along a narrow road, one that led north from the town to the main highway.

It was a clear moonlit night. From the Great Sea a cool breeze came sweeping over the crest of the hills, playing with the wisps of smoke that rose from a hundred dying campfires. Many of the merchants, unable to find lodgings at the inn, had pitched their tents in the open.

Suddenly, without pausing, the girl slackened her pace and allowed Arnon to draw alongside her.

"I am Tirza," she began. "I live with the Prophetess. It is to her home you are being taken. This much I can tell you, and no more."

Arnon's heart leaped. Not in his wildest dreams had he expected to meet the Prophetess face to face! But why? And in the middle of the night? And how did this girl Tirza know where to find him?

Out of the corner of his eye, Arnon tried to get a better look at his companion. The hood of Tirza's cloak dropped over her forehead down to her brow, but Arnon could make out an oval face that curved to a firm chin. Her voice was husky, like the rustling of a warm wind in the hills of Galilee, he thought.

The shadow of a wall loomed ahead, a few paces off to one side of the road. Without slackening pace, Tirza led the way to a gate. It creaked slightly at her touch, and immediately a ball of dark fur came bounding at them out of the darkness.

"Quiet, Navhan," whispered Tirza, giving the huge dog an affectionate pat. "Go tell Deborah we are here."

The dog streaked off toward the house. A thin light shone through a shuttered window.

Tirza pushed open a door. "Please enter," she said.

Arnon found himself in a small entryway which led into a large square room, curtained off at the far end. Simple home-spun tapestries covered the walls. A low divan ran in front of the open fireplace, and gleaming brass ornaments shone in the light of the crackling logs.

At the fireplace stood Deborah, the Prophetess. Her

face was turned toward the door and she smiled faintly as she saw Arnon, standing shakily in the doorway.

So overwhelmed was Arnon by the presence of the Prophetess that he did not even see the two men seated on the divan, until one of them laughed softly. Startled by the familiar ring, Arnon gaped at the man facing him. It was Benjamin. The dust and grime of the afternoon were gone, as were the tattered garments which he had worn when Arnon first saw him on the highway.

"We meet again, Arnon," he called out merrily, much amused by the blank look on the boy's face. "I am happy to see you once more."

But Arnon was scarcely listening. His eyes had shifted to the back of the man still sitting on the divan. There was no mistaking the thick, broad shoulders and the unruly hair, slightly streaked with gray, that curled tightly at the nape of the neck.

"Fa-father!" exclaimed the boy.

Barak rose slowly and walked toward his son, arms extended in greeting. "Welcome, Arnon," he said simply. "You are surprised, but all this will be explained to you. But first bid peace to the Prophetess."

Arnon stepped forward and lowered his head. Deborah placed her hand lightly on his dark hair. "Blessed be your coming and your going," she said softly. "Peace and honor light your path, and the God of our fathers be with you in all that you do." She raised Arnon's chin until her eyes looked deeply into his. "It is indeed an honor," she said finally, "to have in my home the commander of the forces of

Israel *and* his son."

Arnon's jaw dropped. "The commander... of *what?*" he blurted out.

Benjamin's laughter rippled through the room. "One cannot trust these wool merchants, eh, Arnon? Some of them just aren't what they are supposed to be, Arnon."

Barak put his arm around his son's shoulders and led him to the divan. "The time has come for us to talk, my son," he began. "For many years now we of Naftali and Zevulun have been oppressed by the Canaanites of Hazor. It has taken us all that time to learn that this fate is also our punishment, because our people have forsaken the God of our fathers. Yet, God has not abandoned us. In His mercy, though we still do not deserve it, He has sent us a leader to revive our spirits and raise our hopes. And now the word of God has told her that the time has come for us to throw off the Canaanite yoke."

Arnon, eyes glowing, stole a look at the Prophetess.

"Though I am worthy neither of the honor nor of the privilege," Barak went on, "I have been told by the Prophetess that I am to lead the tribes of Israel against King Jabin and Sisera. The time has now come for me to carry out this task."

Arnon's heart was thumping so violently that he pressed his arm against his side. His father... the commander of the tribes of Israel!

"We are about to gather our forces," Barak continued. "Soon messengers will be speeding forth to the chieftains of the tribes with a call for men and arms.

But there is more to our plan, and this is where you will become a part of it."

Arnon gulped hard.

"We are in no position," Barak went on, "to seek out the Canaanites and offer them battle. Therefore, the word of the Lord is that they must be drawn to seek us out. This will not be easy. The Canaanites will not easily be led to believe that we are planning a revolt, since they hold us too weak for any such venture. Yet they must *come* to believe it. We must prick their pride, tempt their boldness, arouse their anger. This is to be the bait in the trap. And for this we must have certain of our people mingle with them, especially in their capital city of Hazor."

Arnon, his eyes bright, was listening to every word. "And... and am I to go to Hazor?" he asked.

Barak nodded. "Yes, my son, You are to go to Hazor. A full-grown man will not succeed where a young lad may, in the plan that we have for this purpose. Though you will not be alone in Hazor, you will face the greatest danger. But you must spread the rumor of a Hebrew uprising. It is for this that I arranged to have your grandfather bring you to Ramah, so that you may receive your orders in the presence of the Prophetess."

"The God of our fathers will watch over you and make you his messenger," Deborah added warmly, "and we shall pray for your safety."

Arnon looked about the room, his eyes searching for Tirza. He had almost forgotten about her in his excitement. She was sitting on a cushion, wordlessly.

Benjamin's voice broke the silence. "You understand now, Arnon," he was saying, "that our meeting on the highway was not quite by accident. A companion and I were riding our horses along the ridge above you until you stopped for your meal."

Barak chuckled. "I know all about your little tussle with the Canaanite charioteer, my son," he said, "and I am not at all displeased by the manner in which you handled him."

For once Benjamin's voice was without merriment. "That fellow won't forget it," he observed soberly. "Let us hope that your paths will never cross again." He was about to say something more but quickly changed his mind.

Barak drew a deep breath. "This is the plan, Arnon. Tomorrow the caravan bearing the tax gift from the merchants of Ramah Market to King Jabin will leave the market place for the royal court. You will be part of that caravan, as the apprentice of one of the camel drivers. But once inside Hazor you will be on your own, my son, and it will be your task to carry out your mission as best as you can."

"A difficult task indeed," commented Benjamin, "yet so important to our cause that we cannot afford to have it fail."

Barak smiled faintly. "Perhaps I was too hasty, Arnon," he remarked. "You will not be entirely alone. Our friend here will manage to be in touch with you from time to time."

Arnon looked at Benjamin. If a full-grown man could not safely go to Hazor, then how...

"Perhaps the boy should be told the whole truth," Benjamin suggested.

"You are right," Barak said. "Arnon, the real name of this man whom you know as Benjamin is Heber. He is a Kenite, a descendant of Jethro, the father-in-law of Moses, the great leader who brought forth our people from Egypt."

Again amazement spread over Arnon's face. "You mean — he is not even an Israelite," he exclaimed, "yet he is fighting for us! Why?"

Not only for you, but with you," Heber told him gently. "You see, Arnon, my tribesmen are few in number, therefore they must live at peace with the Canaanites. Yet the time may come when Jabin — and especially Sisera — will want to conquer more and more peoples. When that time comes, the Kenites may feel the whip of oppression. I have therefore chosen to cast my lot with you, for your victory will be ours, too."

Barak placed his hand on Heber's shoulder. "I hope you will never have cause to regret your decision, dear friend," he said. "I know that your own people are not pleased with it."

Heber shrugged. "Yes, you are right," he agreed. "My people are angry. They are content to live from one day to the next, as long as they are left alone. Some day, perhaps, they will be warriors. But my duty is to fight for them, now, even though they have turned away from me and I from them."

"You have your wife, Yael," Deborah remarked, breaking her long silence.

Heber's dark face brightened. "Yes, I have Yael, and the two of us dwell apart from our people. Still, I am concerned about the fate of all of them."

Barak straightened up. "Very well, then. We shall begin our preparations tomorrow at daybreak. Arnon, you will wait in the courtyard of the inn until a man wearing the striped coat of a caravan leader will come and stand by the gate. His name is Nissan, and you will do as he tells you. Heber will head south to rally the tribe of Reuben. We must make *all* the tribes feel that this is *their* fight. I shall return to Kedesh to meet with the elders of Naftali and Zevulun..."

Barak's words were interrupted by a loud barking outside, followed by a yelp of pain and the gruff sound of men's voices. Instantly Tirza was on her feet, hurrying to the door. Barak and the others, at Deborah's gesture, slipped through the curtain into the dark room beyond.

"It is the Canaanite captain and the guards," came Tirza's voice.

Through the narrow slit in the curtain, Arnon saw a stocky, round-faced guardsman stride into the main chamber. Behind him, in full armor, were three other men.

"In the name of the mighty Jabin, King of Canaan, I greet you," began the captain. His voice, Arnon noted, was as oily as his face.

"The greetings of the King are welcome and pleasing to the ear," replied Deborah. She did not move from her place by the fire. "I trust that everything went well at the Market today, especially since Prince

Etzer was kind enough to pay us a visit."

A look of annoyance crossed the captain's face, but he laughed lightly, showing two rows of small, sharp teeth. "Indeed, everyone has been most orderly. Also, I was pleased to note so much finery in the stalls. It speaks well for the skills of your people."

"It also speaks well for the tax gift that will be going to Hazor tomorrow," Deborah commented coldly.

The captain glanced around the room, and for a moment his eyes rested on the drawn curtain. "We have been making the rounds to see that everything is quiet," he said slowly. "Above all, King Jabin wants peace. You know that, do you not?"

"Peace is indeed a blessing," replied Deborah. "To be left at peace, without being disturbed by people intruding into one's home, is much to be desired. Why is it, then, that you have chosen to come here at this hour of night?"

The captain drew back stiffly. "We have orders to protect you," he said. "King Jabin says that your welfare is very important."

Deborah's lips smiled in scorn. "King Jabin is most kind," she said. "Yet from whom would he have you protect me? Certainly not from my own people."

"No, indeed," said the captain. "Except that there may be fools among them, fools and troublemakers and hotheads who do not understand that all King Jabin wants is peace." His voice became sugary. "Still, we all know that you will not let your people be led astray by wild schemes, eh? After all, there is Sisera, and he has nine hundred iron chariots. What can withstand him, I ask you?"

"Nothing, nothing at all, I am sure," Deborah replied sharply. "And now that you have done your duty and seen to my welfare, I bid you good night."

The captain laughed lightly. During his conversation with Deborah he had been casting long looks at Tirza. "Since there is peace between us," he said, "let there be a little friendliness as well. This week will see King Jabin's birthday, and we shall be holding a little festival tomorrow." He turned to Tirza. "You may come to the festival, as my own guest," he added grandly.

Tirza eyed the Canaanite calmly. "I do not deserve this honor," she said, "nor do I want it."

The captain's face grew dark and he said with a menacing scowl: "Proud are you, my pretty maiden?" advancing a step toward the girl.

One of the Canaanite guards reached out a restraining hand. "Be not rash, Captain," he whispered. "Better let us depart."

The captain bit his lip in anger, then savagely turned on his heel and left the house, his men close behind him. Arnon heard Navhan's low growl and the creak of the gate. A moment later everything was quiet.

Deborah blew out the candle, leaving the room dark except for the glow in the fireplace. Then she pulled the curtain aside.

Barak heaved a deep sigh. "Our revolt was no more than a hair's breadth from breaking out, right then and there," he said. "Had that Canaanite taken another step toward Tirza we would have come out, daggers in hand."

"I wonder whether the Canaanites suspect anything," Heber put in.

"Tyrants — and their servants — always do," Deborah remarked wearily, sitting down on the divan. A faint smile came to her lips. "In this case, though, I suspect that the Canaanite was more interested in asking Tirza to come to the festival than in any Hebrew plot against his King Jabin."

Barak was still not satisfied. "Are you sure that no harm will come to you?"

Deborah laughed lightly. "Do not fear for my safety, Barak," she said. "I am the reason the Canaanites feel sure that our people will not revolt. After all, the Hebrews have but a woman to lead them." A faraway look came into her eyes. "Little does King Jabin know that his defeat will come at the hands of a woman — and that the woman may not be Deborah the Prophetess!"

CHAPTER THREE

ADVENTURE IN HAZOR

The councilmen of Ramah tried their best to bring an air of light-heartedness and festivity into the Spring Market, and, indeed, it was gay and colorful — until the final day came, and with it a change in the mood of the people. The market place itself overflowed with people, but there was little buying or selling. This was Tax Day.

King Jabin had craftily decreed that the tax gift for the royal court was to be collected not on the first day of the Market but on the last, when the finest and most expensive wares would still be unsold (for who would be foolish enough to buy them and show that he was wealthy ?). Any merchant caught holding his wares back would be put to death, by order of the King.

Tax Day was always the same. Early in the morning the Canaanite tax collector, accompanied by a squad of guardsmen and several carts, would proceed from stall to stall and point to whatever caught his fancy. All the wares which he thus selected would be placed in the carts and taken to the waiting camels for the caravan to Hazor.

The tax collector, a short, scrawny man by the name of Masrosh, was hated and feared by all the merchants. He had the eye of an eagle and his bony finger darted from one fine item to another, as though he had studied each one and was familiar with its value. The merchants kept their eyes averted as Masrosh approached their stalls, knowing well that he could easily deprive them of their entire profit, or even cause them heavy losses, if he so chose.

The crowd in the market place filed slowly past in the wake of Masrosh and his train of guards and carts. There was complete silence, broken only by a gasp or a murmur when Masrosh's finger almost emptied a stall here and there.

The sun was already high in the heavens when Masrosh finally came to the last stall, where the camel caravan was stationed. Hot and perspiring from his arduous task, the tax collector retired to a seat prepared for him in the shade and devoted himself to a long narrow pitcher. But he kept his eyes on the wares he had gathered which were now being transferred from the carts to crates atop the camels.

One of the camel drivers was Arnon, but even his closest friends in Kedesh would have found him hard to recognize. His usually neat hair hung in straggling wisps over his smudged forehead. Over his shoulder was draped the shapeless, loose, ankle-length cloak of the camel driver's apprentice, and his voice, as he grunted to the camels to stand still while the crates were being loaded, was rasping and unpleasant.

The boy had slept little after returning to the inn. The thought of the mission to Hazor had kept him awake for a good hour. Just one day earlier he had been a carefree lad, excited about his first Spring Market, and now the very fate of his people might be in his hands ! He thrilled at the thought. Even Barak's warning that, if found out, the best he could expect would be a quick death did not dampen his spirits. To strike for his people's freedom from the Canaanite yoke was the most important thing in the world, worth any sacrifice.

Neither Barak nor Heber was on hand in the market place to witness the tax collection. Both were gone when dawn broke over Ramah. As for Deborah, it was known that she would not leave her house the entire day. The townspeople well remembered her reply when King Jabin had asked her to be present at the collection, to show the people that she approved of the tax. "O King," the Prophetess had replied, loud enough for all to hear, "the God of my people has set me to judge between men. This tax is yours not by right but by force. I shall not give my hand to it." The Canaanite ruler was much angered by the reply, Arnon had heard, but he did not dare to punish the Prophetess.

Neither was Tirza to be seen on Tax Day, and Arnon sadly wondered whether he would ever see her again.

By mid-afternoon, the caravan, under guard of a detachment of Canaanite soldiers, was on its way to

Jabin's capital. Arnon was the only apprentice. The three others were well-trained camel drivers who had made the journey several times before. Masrosh himself, his work done, had already departed in his chariot for Hazor with the list of the fine items he had collected at the Ramah Spring Market.

Arnon's heart began to beat faster as he recognized the lane into which the caravan was turning. It was the same along which Tirza had led him the night before to Deborah's house. Yes, King Jabin was a crafty one! Since the Prophetess would not come to the market place for the tax collection, the caravan was ordered to pass by her house on its way out of the town.

There was the house, around a bend in the lane. Arnon thought he heard a dog's bark, but he was not sure. No sign of life came from beyond the gate. Arnon lowered his eyes and kept plodding beside his camel.

Late in the evening the head of the detachment ordered a halt. In the distance, lights were twinkling, and suddenly Arnon realized that the caravan had stopped on the outskirts of his native town of Kedesh. In the darkness he could still "see" the scenes he knew so well — the sloping streets, the town square, the patches where the small children played "watch-your-station."

"Very peaceful, isn't it?" said a voice at Arnon's side.

It was Nissan, the leader of the caravan, who had called for Arnon early that morning. The boy had taken a liking at once to the burly, black-bearded Nissan, whose passive face revealed nothing of what was in his heart.

"We shall be in Hazor tomorrow," Nissan continued, keeping his voice low. "Before then, we shall have to put into play the plan that will make it possible for you to remain there."

"My father has much faith in you," Arnon remarked.

Nissan waved the words away. "Barak gives me more than is my due, but I am pleased by the faith that he has in me." He looked around carefully. The Canaanite guards, having finished their supper, were sprawled on the grass around the dying campfire "While I still have to figure out what our final plan will be, this much is certain : whatever we do in Hazor to get you to remain there will have to be done in public."

Arnon cocked his head. "What do you mean ?"

"Simply this," returned Nissan. "You cannot remain in Hazor for no reason at all. Neither can you stay there in hiding, for that will not achieve the purpose of your being there. You must find your way to King Jabin's court itself, and there try to spread the rumor about the coming Hebrew revolt. The Canaanites must be drawn to attack our men on Mount Tabor : so says the Prophetess."

Arnon whistled softly in the darkness. "I wonder," he mused, "which will turn out to be the more difficult task, working up some excuse to stay at Hazor or having the Canaanites believe my story !"

Nissan grunted. "I have something in mind. By the time we reach Hazor I hope to have it all worked out. Right now we had better get some sleep. Our guards will no doubt want to arrive in the city as early as possible."

Nissan had guessed correctly. The first streaks of dawn were hardly visible on the crest of the hills to the east when the caravan was already on its way. About two hours' distance from the Canaanite capital, it was met by a herald in a chariot. After a few words with the guards, he wheeled about and headed back to Hazor to announce the arrival of the caravan and give the townspeople enough time to get to the gate as the camels filed through into the city itself.

Arnon, following the example of the other drivers, looked neither to right nor left, although he was very curious to see Hazor. In Kedesh it was said that the Canaanite capital was a glorious place indeed.

The caravan was now at the entrance to the palace grounds. The courtyard itself, Arnon saw, was almost big enough to hold the entire throng that had been following at the heels of the caravan all through the city.

The courtyard ended at a broad stone terrace that ran along the entire front of the palace. At the edge of the terrace, surrounded by his ministers, sat King Jabin, his fleshy, heavy features glowing with pleasure. In his pudgy hand he held the list which Masrosh, stationed to his left, had given him. The King must already have been thinking of the brilliant new cloaks he would soon have, although the royal attire which he was now wearing was so bright with ornaments that the camels, accustomed as they were to the blinding light of the sun, were yet dazzled by the glitter.

In contrast to Masrosh and Jabin himself, the man at the King's right was large of bone and of towering stature. Despite the heat of the day he wore on his head an iron helmet which perfectly suited his hawk-like nose, thin, tighly-drawn lips and wiry beard. Around his wrist he wore a wide leather thong to which was attached a long, iron-studded whip.

This man was General Sisera, feared as no other warrior throughout the entire land of Canaan and far beyond its borders. His power was boundless, for with his iron chariots he was master of the land. Fortunately for King Jabin, Sisera was a warrior who disdained anything that did not smack of battle, and the thought of ruling Canaan from the throne never entered his mind. For this, too, King Jabin was grateful; Sisera was not of royal blood, but he was powerful enough to do whatever he wanted.

Sisera's dark face remained unchanged as a wide carpet was rolled out at King Jabin's feet and the palace servants began unloading the baskets. As each armful was heaped on the carpet, however, his expression changed. A strange light came into his eyes as he gazed at the fine cloth, silver-lined leather craft and metal ornaments that kept spilling over onto the carpet. At one point, he bent down and muttered something into the King's ear. To Arnon, watching closely, it seemed that, for a fleeting instant, the smile disappeared from Jabin's face.

41

The boy's eyes roved over the others on the terrace and suddenly he gave such a start that Nissan shot him a warning glance. Arnon lowered his head and looked again. He was not mistaken. Almost directly behind King Jabin, the stern features of Prince Etzer stood out clearly. Arnon had recognized the Canaanite nobleman whose chariot had smashed Avinoam's cart on the Kedesh-Ramah highway.

Although Arnon was aware of Nissan's questioning look, he dared not make a move. If the Prince were to recognize him in turn, there might be a few questions to answer — and his whole mission would be doomed!

Just then the bugle sounded, marking the end of the show. The gathering on the terrace stirred and parted to make way for the procession of servants as they carried the finery to the royal treasure house. King Jabin rose from his throne, a broad smile wreathing his round face. As for the crowd, every man cheered lustily even though none of the townspeople in the courtyard would ever get a thread of all that finery for his own household.

The last servant and the last armful disappeared into the palace, and the crowd began to disperse slowly. Those nearest the caravan remained behind long enough to hurl a few choice taunts at the silent Israelite drivers.

"We are now free to leave," murmured Nissan to Arnon, as he prodded his camel to its feet. "It is time for me to tell you our plan of action."

Arnon moved closer, pretending to help Nissan with his reluctant animal.

"When we get to the market place," Nissan said, "you and I will appear to engage in a bitter quarrel about the wages I am supposed to be paying you. I shall knock you down, take your camel and walk away. You will proceed to curse me, my tribe, my ancestors, and any one else you wish to think of. I am sure that the Canaanites of Hazor will egg you on, for nothing pleases them more than to see an Israelite turn against his own people."

"And after that," commented Arnon, "I shall be on my own."

"Exactly," Nissan said. "I will pay no attention to you; neither will the other drivers. We shall simply leave Hazor. As for you, someone is bound to take kindly to you, especially when you begin talking about an Israelite uprising. But don't let yourself be questioned too much, at first. Insist on telling your story only to some high official — King Jabin himself, perhaps."

Arnon pulled his camel into line. "And Heber will be here in a few days?"

"If all goes well, yes," replied Nissan. "His is a most difficult mission, too, but we have high hopes." He lowered his voice. "We are approaching the market place. When we draw abreast the sandalmaker's stall yonder, you will begin to lag behind. Ten paces farther, I shall turn around and begin to berate you for your laziness. The rest you know."

Arnon began counting the paces to the stall: fifty ... twenty-five ... twenty ... fifteen ... ten ...

Just as the two Israelites were about to carry out

their plan, a rumbling noise topped by cries of dismay and alarm came to their ears. An instant later, a chariot drawn by two wild-eyed horses came clattering down the main road to the market place. In the chariot, clinging frantically to the side of the swaying vehicle, was a little boy.

Far behind the chariot, hardly visible in the cloud of dust, a burly figure was giving futile chase to the runaways. Others now took up the pursuit. In another moment, the chariot would crash into the first row of stalls.

As the onrushing chariot drew near, Arnon braced himself, facing in the direction the horses were heading. Before Nissan could reach out a restraining hand, Arnon leaped straight at the surging animals.

For a split second it seemed that the brave youth would be trampled beneath the flying hooves. Luckily, Arnon's last step had bounced him off the ground at exactly the right angle. His fingers dug into the mane of the horse nearest him. The next instant he was astride the animal and tugging at the reins. The two horses reared, pawed, and shuddered to a halt.

Arnon slid shakily to the ground, hardly aware of the cheers of the fast-gathering crowd. In the meantime a dozen hands lifted the little boy, limp with fright, from the chariot.

Arnon looked about for Nissan. Their plan had gone astray. Or had it ? While the caravan leader was nowhere in sight, Arnon now saw only too well who it was that had come in pursuit of the chariot, and his heart skipped a beat. It was Nehag, Prince Etzer's notorious charioteer.

"Make way! Make way!" Nehag was shouting, as he clawed his way through the surging crowd. "Keep back! Let no one touch the boy!" The charioteer's voice, hoarse with dust, could hardly be heard above the excited tumult.

Suddenly another chariot came clattering into the market place. Its driver leaped to the ground before the horse had come to a halt. "Stand aside!" he cried.

The tumult died away as if by magic. Nehag stopped his clawing, and a look of fear came to his sweat-streaked face.

"It is Prince Etzer," a murmur ran through the crowd.

The Prince shouldered his way to the chariot and swept the lad up into his arms. "What happened, my son?" he asked.

The youngster, still pale with fright, embraced his father tightly. "I was bad," he said, so faintly that only those around the chariot could hear the words. "Nehag was not in the yard, so I climbed up... and the horses ran away."

Nehag managed to wriggle through until he reached his master's side. "I went to get a new harness, Your Highness," he blurted. "I couldn't have been gone more than a few..."

"I did not ask for an explanation," the Prince cut him off. He turned to the boy. "What happened then?"

"The horses kept running and running," the lad replied. "Then suddenly they stopped. I looked up, and there was someone on Black Pride's back."

"Here he is, Your Highness," came shouts from the crowd, and Arnon, wiping away the perspiration that streaked his face, felt himself being pushed toward the Canaanite nobleman.

Prince Etzer lowered his son gently into the chariot and turned to face the boy's rescuer. Immediately a gleam of recognition came into his eyes.

"So! The young man of the splintered cart!" he exclaimed. "Is there not enough adventure where you come from that you should seek it in Hazor?"

Arnon reddened. "It was mere chance, Your Highness," he returned. "I was hired for the caravan that brought the tax from Ramah." He looked about in feigned alarm. "My camel! What has happened to my camel?"

The Prince smiled, and at this a pleased titter ran through the crowd. The lad was an Israelite true enough, but he had pluck, by Baal!

"So you came with the gifts to the King," Prince Etzer went on, "and to me you brought one as well— the life of my son. I want to reward you for what you have done, at the risk of your own life." He reached inside his cloak, as though groping for a purse, then changed his mind. "You seem to have much skill in handling horses," he said slowly, "even though you are a camel driver. I want you to teach my son how to handle them. You will remain in Hazor and be his tutor."

Arnon's heart leaped, but his face remained calm. This was too good to be true! "It is indeed an honor,

Your Highness," he said, "but what will my father say? And what about my camel?"

Loud laughter broke from the onlookers. A jester indeed, this Israelite lad! To be thinking of a camel when he was being offered a place at the royal court!

"Your father, unless he is a fool, will be greatly pleased," the Prince said. Over the heads in the crowd, he caught sight of one of the Israelite drivers, with his camel by him. "You, there!" the Prince cried. "Come here at once!"

Nissan shuffled forward. He kept his eyes low, but Arnon knew that there was gladness in his heart.

"You know this boy's father?" Prince Etzer demanded.

Nissan nodded. "Yes, Your Highness," he replied. "A wool merchant he is, a poor man who will bless Your Highness for having given his son such a high position."

"There!" cried the Prince, placing his hand on Arnon's shoulder. "It is as I thought. Your father will be overjoyed when he hears about your good fortune."

A cheer went up from the crowd. Prince Etzer smiled and motioned to Arnon to get into his chariot. As the boy turned to obey, he happened to meet Nehag's eyes, and in them he saw black hatred.

CHAPTER FOUR

HEBER'S MISSION FAILS

On the same morning that the gift tax caravan completed its journey to Hazor, Heber the Kenite was making preparation for his own mission.

He awoke early and glanced about the tent in the half-light. Yael, his wife, was already up; he could hear her outside the tent, preparing the morning meal. For a moment he remained lying on the straw mat, his eyes closed.

When was the first time that he had seen Yael? To Heber it seemed like yesterday, when he beheld her at a festive gathering of the Kenite clan to which he belonged — a quiet young girl from a southern branch of the tribe, beautiful to look at, but strange ... a girl, people said, who could look into the future and see the evil in it ... it was for this reason, they said, that none of the young men would ask for her hand in marriage. Heber, handsome, full of life, the best horseman in the clan, laughed and said all that talk was nonsense; Yael might see evil in the future, but he could see no evil in her. And if the other young men were fools, so much the better for him.

And so Heber lost no time. He went to his own family and told his kinfolk that he had in mind to take a wife. At this, they all were overjoyed, but when he told them that it was Yael whom he wanted to marry, he was met with stony silence. The girl was considered almost a witch! But Heber did not falter, not even when his father refused to give his consent. Heber mounted his horse and rode south. Fortunately for him, Yael's father, afraid that no one would ever ask for her hand, was willing to give her away in marriage for a small dowry. The two were married, but Yael was not made welcome by her husband's family. After a brief but unpleasant time in their midst, Heber took his wife and pitched their tent far from the others and there they lived, quietly. They never talked about what the future would hold.

The fragrance of freshly-baked bread came to Heber's nostrils. He rose quickly, dipped his face into the full basin in a corner of the tent and went outside, where Yael was bent over her task. He stole up silently and pinched the lobe of her ear. She turned her face up to him, her dark eyes glowing in the morning light.

"Will you be gone long?" she asked.

"Two days, not more," Heber replied. For a moment there was silence between them. The Kenite drew a deep breath. "We are coming upon hard times," he said. "Perhaps it is better that I take you to your kinfolk in the south."

"I shall stay here," Yael said. Her voice trembled a little, a sign which Heber knew to mean that her mind was on things yet to come. "The flock needs tending. No one will harm me."

Breakfast over, Heber filled his water skin and put it, along with the food that Yael had prepared, into his saddle bags. A moment later he was cantering east, toward the Jordan.

He reached the River and began following its winding course down the green valley, riding at an easy canter along the grassy bank. Twice he led his mount off the beaten trail in order to avoid caravans coming toward him from the south. He had neither the time nor the desire to stop for a chat.

North of Jericho, its walls still in ruins from the days of Joshua, Heber crossed the Jordan to the eastern bank and into Reubenite territory.

The tribe of Reuben, along with that of Gad and half of Manasseh, had chosen to settle east of the Jordan many years earlier, when the Israelites, under the leadership of Moses, were still on their way from Egyptian bondage to the Promised Land. The warriors of these tribes had helped the others to conquer Canaan, west of the River, as they had promised to do. When this was done they returned east to their own families.

In time, the tribes built new towns and villages, for their numbers kept growing with each generation. Still, their largest towns were those which they had wrested from the Amorites when those enemies of old had attempted to bar the way of the advancing tribes of Israel.

Heber's destination was Baal-Meon, one of the for-

mer Amorite centers. To avoid traveling in the heat of the day, the Kenite turned off the road to a shady spot, ate a light meal and lay down for a nap.

But sleep did not come easily. Deborah's last words to him kept turning over and over in Heber's mind. "As long as the separate tribes of Israel look only to their own needs," the Prophetess had said, "there will never be a *people* of Israel. Whatever threatens one tribe must be of concern to the others, otherwise their enemies will overcome them, one by one, one after the other."

It was for this reason that Deborah and Barak were sending messengers to all the outlying tribes, even those untouched by the rule of the Canaanites, with the call to join their brethren to the north in the uprising against Jabin.

Heber accepted his mission without a word but, being wise in the ways of men, he had his doubts. If Naftali and Zevulun, dwelling in the midst of the Canaanites and oppressed as they were by Jabin, had shown no desire to risk a revolt, what could be expected of the others? The tribes of Dan and Asher, in the territories just a few hours' distance away toward the setting sun, had already been approached, and they showed little desire to answer the call to arms; indeed, at the first sign of danger they would probably board their ships and sail beyond harm's reach. As for the southern tribes, it was all they could do to keep the warlike Philistines at bay.

Still, Heber could understand the Prophetess and her reasons. If only two or three other tribes — especially the Reubenites, the descendants of Jacob's eldest son — would join in the uprising, then *all* the tribes would be better off, for their enemies would think twice before attacking a united people. Yes, it was worth the effort.

Late in the afternoon, Heber arose and continued on his way across the grassy plain. Looking about the fertile countryside, he could well understand why the Reubenites had chosen to remain here. The grass was like a thick carpet underfoot. Herds of cattle dotted the scene with their brown and white patches, and flocks of fat sheep browsed on the gently sloping hillsides. The warm air itself breathed peace and contentment.

The Kenite reached the outskirts of Baal-Meon well before dusk. His destination was the home of Shimshi, Barak's good friend and one of the chieftains of Reuben. But instead of heading for Shimshi's dwelling. Heber wen on to the market place.

The stalls were doing a brisk business. The hum of voices filled the air, rising high to bargain and dropping low for a bit of gossip. All around was lightness of heart. Not one word did Heber hear about the northern tribes and their plight.

Heber finally asked to be directed to Shimshi's house. At the entrance he was met by the chieftain himself.

"You wish to see me?" asked Shimshi, eyeing the newcomer. "Where do you come from and for whom will you speak?"

In answer Heber went down on one knee. With a

twig he scratched into the soft earth the outline of a sheep, then drew a broken thunderbolt line through it. This was the sign of Barak, the wool merchant of Kedesh.

Immediately a warm smile came to Shimshi's face. "If it is from my friend Barak that you come," he exclaimed, "be welcome indeed! Enter my home."

Once inside, Heber gratefully accepted the pitcher of cool water and joined his host on the soft sheepskin rug. Shimshi listened intently as the Kenite, speaking with quiet earnestness, told him the nature of his mission.

"It is as you say, my friend," the Reubenite chieftain sighed, when Heber fell silent. "Today the Canaanites of Hazor are oppressing our brethren of Naftali and Zevulun. Tomorrow the heavy hand of the Philistines may lay itself on Judah and Benjamin. Around us the Amorites, though not troublesome today, may arouse others to attack us. But at present there is peace in the land. Food is plentiful, and when the stomach is full the heart is lulled."

Heber had expected to hear something like this, still he could not hide his disappointment. "Then it is your opinion, O Shimshi, that the tribal chieftains of Reuben will turn a deaf ear to the words of the Prophetess herself?"

Again Shimshi sighed. "I know them well, my fellow chieftains," he replied sadly, "and I know what their answer will be. Yet I shall not speak for them. Since it is the command of the Prophetess and the wish of my friend Barak, I shall gather them to listen to your words at sunrise tomorrow. Perhaps the spirit of the Prophetess will move them. Until then, my home is yours."

At dawn on the following day Heber was startled out of his sleep by a sound such as he had never heard before in his life. It seemed to come from the courtyard, and Heber, draping himself hastily in his cloak, went to the door and cautiously peered out. There, squatting on the cool earth, their eyes still heavy with sleep, were some ten or eleven children. Each one was clutching a reed pipe and, under the direction of a youth standing over the group, was tootling for all he was worth. The result was an eerie wail that sounded to Heber like the cry of a jackal tumbling down a cliff. The Kenite shook his head and headed for the wash basin.

Shimshi was much amused when Heber told him about the incident. "We are accustomed to these sounds," he laughed. "You must understand, my dear friend, that our children grow up with two goals: to be skilled shepherds and to excel with the shepherd's pipe. They begin preparing for these goals very early, early in life and early in the morning."

Heber shrugged. "We too raise sheep, up north," he commented, "but not with the fervor that you do here! Of course," he added, "our land up there is nowhere near as good for grazing as the well-watered plains of Reuben."

Shimshi glanced at the sun. The chieftains of Reuben would soon be gathering at the gates of Baal-Meon where he was to meet them and afterwards escort them to his home.

"You will wait here," he said to Heber, "for it is the custom of the host to meet his guests alone." For a moment he hesitated, as though trying to find the right words for what he wanted to say. "Do not ask them for too much," he remarked, "else you will not gain their ears. If they refuse to send warriors, they may still agree to supply your men with food."

"Ha, food!" snorted Heber to himself, although he said nothing. What would Barak do with it? Feed Sisera's horses to death?

Shimshi knew his chieftains well indeed. After Heber had spoken to the men seated in the shady part of the courtyard, there was much talk about the need for peace. Finally, the Reubenites came to a decision: warriors, definitely no; food, yes, but it would have to be carted away during the night, so that the Canaanites would get no wind of the act.

"Your offer, I know, comes from the bottom of your hearts," Heber pointed out, striving mightily to keep both anger and sarcasm out of his voice, "but it is not food that we need. The revolt against Jabin will have to be short and swift; the few hours between meals may decide the fate of the northern tribes for years to come. It is warriors we must have, as many as we can muster. Then, too, with you Reubenites fighting alongside your kinsmen of Naftali and Zevulun, victory will also bring unity, just as it did when your forefathers fought alongside the other tribes to conquer the land under Joshua!"

"Ha, that is right!" one of the younger chieftains

cried. "But in those days our warriors *had* to do it because Moses had made them promise that they would cross the Jordan. We today have made no such promise. If the other tribes are too weak to hold their own against the Canaanites or the Philistines, that is their problem, not ours."

Loud cries of approval greeted his words.

"Also," added another chieftain, "why will you not tell us your plan of battle ? If we like it, and if we think that it will bring you victory..."

"Only a fool would promise victory before the battle," snapped Heber, his patience beginning to wear thin. "Besides, is not the word of the Prophetess enough when she says that the God of your fathers will be with you ?"

The chieftain spread his hands in triumph. "Very well, then," he exclaimed. "If the Prophetess is sure of the help of God, why come to us for the help of men ?"

"That is right !" came from the circle.

Shimshi raised his hand to silence the group. "To me the words of the Prophetess are clear," he said slowly. "It will take a miracle to defeat Sisera and, therefore, God *will have to be* with the tribes. But to deserve a miracle such as this, not only Naftali and Zevulun but we their brethren as well must be willing to face the danger. Otherwise we shall not be worthy of witnessing the might of God's hand."

A growl of displeasure came from the chieftains, but before anyone could say a word there again came the wailing of the shepherd's pipes. As if by magic, the scowls disappeared from the faces of the Reubenite leaders and pleased smiles took their place. To judge from their look of rapture, the chieftains were listening to a host of heaven's angels.

"The children of Baal-Meon learn quickly," one of them congratulated Shimshi. "They should do well at the piping contest next month."

Heber could restrain himself no longer. He leaped to his feet and glared at the startled Reubenites.

"You are men with the hearts of sheep," he cried out in disgust, "and your eyes are blinded by their wool. Your ears open in delight to the sound of the shepherd's pipe but they are closed to the pleading of your brethren!"

Shimshi, his face red with shame, bowed his head.

"It is just as well," the Kenite continued, tightening the girdle about his cloak. "Men with hearts of sheep are worse than no men at all."

And with this he left the courtyard.

CHAPTER FIVE

THE PLAN GROWS ROOT

Arnon's first few days in Hazor passed without incident.

In Prince Etzer's palace, he was given a spacious room, near the one occupied by little Nasik, his pupil. Here the Israelite youth saw such comforts as he had never imagined. His father's house in Kedesh was one of the finest in the town but, compared with the palace, it was hardly more than a rough stone hut. Fine tapestries adorned the walls and rich skins covered the smooth stone floors. His own room overlooked green groves and beautiful gardens that filled the air with their fragrance.

Arnon's rescue of Nasik endeared him to the entire family, for the lad was the only son of Prince Etzer and his wife, Princess Piria. The boy's parents were even more delighted to see how quickly Nasik became attached to his tutor. Every day the two would mount their horses and go off for their riding lesson in the meadows outside Hazor.

Still not for one moment did Arnon forget the purpose of his being in Hazor. The problem was how and where to begin. Then, on the third day, young Nasik quite innocently furnished him with the opening that he was seeking.

They were riding along the grassy trail toward the hills when Nasik exclaimed, out of the clear sky: "You are not at all like Nehag."

Arnon smiled. "And how am I not like Nehag?," he asked.

"He talks all the time," Nasik replied, "mostly about himself. He thinks that he can handle a chariot better than Sisera." Then a note of pride came into his voice. "But my father is better than Sisera."

"I am sure he is," agreed Arnon, eyeing the boy. "What else does Nehag talk about?"

Nasik laughed. "Everything," he commented. "He says I will never be a charioteer. He thinks I am lazy. If I do something he does not like, off he goes to tell my father about it. But he is that way about the fellows in the stables. The minute he hears them say anything — well, about the hard work they have to do — off he goes to complain to my father."

"So?" remarked Arnon. "How the stable-boys must love him for it!"

The boy broke into laughter. "You should hear the names they call him... when he isn't listening."

"They must be afraid of him," Arnon suggested.

Nasik nodded. "They are. He is very strong. A stable-boy once wrestled with him, and Nehag broke his back. I saw it from behind the stable." The boy shuddered, as if trying to shake off the memory of the terrifying incident.

Nothing more was said. Arnon showed his pupil how to guide a horse down a hilly slope, then the two headed back to town.

How strange, thought Arnon, that a Canaanite child should have given him the idea! He could hardly wait until nightfall.

It was an unusually warm evening. Prince Etzer and his wife had gone up to the roof of the palace to enjoy the evening breeze. Nasik, after a brief hour with Arnon at wood-carving, was fast asleep. Arnon, fully dressed, lay on his cot, and went over the details of his plan. Then he arose and sauntered down to the stables.

As he had expected, Nehag was there with several of the stable-boys. The charioteer, a jug clasped tightly in his thick fingers, was giving an account of one of his daring adventures.

"Behold, your friend comes," Arnon overheard one of the stable-boys mutter.

Nehag threw a quick glance toward the door. "Shut your cursed mouth," he growled, "or you won't have a tooth in it."

Arnon strode past the group into the inner stable. He was back in a moment. "You should keep the outer door open on a hot night like this," he said crisply. "The horses need all the fresh air they can get."

"We haven't heard any complaints from them," one of the boys remarked with a wink.

The others laughed, but on Nehag's face the scowl

deepened. "We don't need a Israelite upstart to tell us how horses should be handled," he snarled, tossing the pitcher aside.

Arnon came nearer. "If you don't like what I say," he said slowly, "you should complain to the Prince. I understand that such is your custom."

A gasp came from the stable-boys. The Israelite youth was indeed looking for trouble!

"Prince Etzer," continued Arnon, outwardly calm, "seems to think that I do know something about horses. If you think that he is wrong, it is your duty to tell him so, is it not?"

Nehag spat viciously into the dust. "Clever one, aren't you?" he cried. "If I had my way, every one of you Israelites would be ground to dust under our chariot wheels."

"That will be a pleasure which you will never live to see," Arnon retorted, seeming to lose all control over himself. "Before long my people will rise up and throw off the Canaanite yoke!"

One of the older stable-men raised his hand. "You are a bold youth to speak such words," he remarked, sharply. "Favored as you may be by our master the Prince, Hazor is not the place to talk of an uprising."

"And what about Sisera's chariots?" another man demanded. "How will your Israelites stop them with their bare hands?"

This was the opening that Arnon needed. "Chariots!" he snorted in derision. "Who has ever heard of chariots going up the side of a mountain?"

A puzzled look came to the faces of the men on the

floor, and the elderly one spoke up again. "A mountain?" he repeated. "What in the name of Baal are you talking about?"

"You see!" retorted Arnon triumphantly. "We Israelites are also wise in the ways of war! Wait till we fortify Mount Tabor and control the main highway! How will your chariots be able to..."

All of a sudden Arnon broke off, as though realizing that he had talked too much. With a mumbled remark about the lateness of the hour he hurried out of the stable.

In the shadows outside the stable Arnon paused to listen. From within came the sounds of excited talk, with Nehag's voice rising above the others. Arnon smiled with satisfaction and went to his room. The next day, he thought, should be most exciting.

He was not wrong. In the morning, back from a ride with Nasik, there was a palace guard waiting for him. He was to appear before King Jabin in the main wing of the palace right away.

Although the Canaanite ruler liked pleasure and comfort, the chamber where he held his meetings on matters of state was bare and sparsely furnished. The throne itself was made of stout wood, covered with leather, with the royal emblem carved into its high back.

The King was seated on this throne, nervously fingering his chin when Arnon entered. At his right sat Sisera, gripping his driver's whip. Like King Jabin, Sisera appeared in ill humor, and he growled audibly when the Israelite youth made his appearance. All this was not lost on the score of councillors who formed a half-circle about their ruler.

Arnon bowed low before the assemblage. His face was the picture of fear and dismay.

At a nod from King Jabin, Prince Etzer leaned forward. "Arnon," he began, "do you have any idea why you have been summoned to appear before the council ?"

Arnon bit his lip and fidgeted. "Y-yes, Your Highness, I do," he replied.

The answer caught the councillors by surprise.

"That oaf Nehag insulted my people," Arnon went on, with well-simulated bravado. "Therefore, I told him that some day they will... well, they will try to become free of Canaanite rule. But that was just talk," he added hastily.

"What about an Israelite plan to fortify Mount Tabor ?" the Prince went on. "Was that just talk, Arnon, or is there something more ?"

The boy allowed a look of amazement to cross his face, then dropped his eyes. "I do not know, Your Highness," he replied slowly. "I heard it last week from the caravan drivers, as we came up from Ramah. But it must be no more than a foolish rumor, for who would dare challenge the might of Commander Sisera and his iron chariots ?"

The scowl on Sisera's face grew uglier. "Tell us more, boy," he cried, "or you won't see another sunrise."

"I know no more," Arnon replied, trembling. "I

heard it said that from Mount Tabor the Israelites would be able to cut off the highway and ambush the chariots as they went by."

A silence fell on the chamber. It was broken suddenly by a crash, as sharp as a thunder clap. Sisera had brought the handle of his whip down upon the heavy table with such force that a splinter flew from the wood. Then he turned toward the King so suddenly that the latter shrank against the high back of the throne.

"Even if this be no more than a rumor," he shouted, "I am ready to wipe out every Israelite man, woman and child within one week in punishment!"

Sudden fear clutched at Arnon's heart. Had he gone too far in prodding Sisera?

Prince Etzer spoke up. "I am afraid that we have allowed ourselves to become concerned over nothing," he remarked. "Let us think about it for a moment. Let us say that the Israelites do gather in force on Mount Tabor. Let us say that they are well-armed. Is it not true that Commander Sisera, by besieging the mountain with his hundreds of chariots, could easily starve the Israelites up there into submission? Yes, they might have food for one week or two, or a month at the most, but in the end they would have to yield. Therefore, why should they even consider such a plan? It is foolhardy."

King Jabin looked at his councillors. Prince Etzer's words had evidently impressed them. "Why the rumor, then?" the King asked.

The Prince shrugged. "I can only guess, sire," he

replied. "It may be that the Israelites are entertaining wild dreams just to keep up their spirits. Of course," he added, "it may not hurt to look a little deeper into this matter."

The King seemed pleased. "True, indeed," he exclaimed. "We must know more about it."

Sisera jerked his head impatiently. "Bah," he cried in disgust. "I say destroy them all and save the trouble. Besides, my warriors have had nothing to do lately. They need action."

Prince Etzer eyed him coldly. "His Majesty has just told us what should be done," he said. "I believe that we have a man who can tell us what we want to know."

"Ah, good!" the King exclaimed, greatly pleased. "Who is this man?"

"One who has always been on good terms with us," replied Prince Etzer. "He is not a Canaanite and can therefore move freely among the Israelites without their knowing what he is up to. He is a Kenite by the name of Heber."

Fortunately for Arnon, the eyes of the councillors were fixed on Prince Etzer, otherwise they would have noticed the startled look on the boy's face. He felt his knees trembling. Heber... a spy for the Canaanites?

Arnon was barely aware that the King was dismissing him from the chamber. He turned about and shakily followed the guard out into the corridor.

A few minutes later the storm which had been brewing in the council chamber broke loose.

It began almost without reason. King Jabin was about to call an end to the meeting when Prince Etzer asked to be heard again.

"I have changed my thinking," he began slowly. "It is quite possible that the Israelites, even though they have no leader..."

"Only a woman," one of the councillors interrupted.

"Although they have no leader," the Prince resumed, "they may have those among them who would try some move against us, to keep up their courage. We should, therefore, take action to discourage any such move. After all, even if the Israelites have no chance of succeeding, a clash at this time will disturb the peace of our own people."

"Come to the point," Sisera called out impatiently. "What do you have in mind?"

The Prince ignored him. "The Mount Tabor scheme sounds like a move that the Israelites might make. Therefore, even though we have chariots on all the highways, I say that we prevent their fortifying Mount Tabor by placing a strong watch along its slopes.

Again Sisera's whip came crashing down on the table. "Fortify Mount Tabor?" he roared. "Do you mean that my chariots need your troops to help them?"

For the first time Prince Etzer became angry. "Do *you* mean," he cried, "that men must be teamed with horses in order to be warriors?"

The councillors sat with bated breath. They were

well aware of the rivalry between Prince Etzer, in command of the Canaanite army, and Sisera, commander of the charioteer corps. Now this rivalry was threatening to break out into an open feud.

Sisera's eyes blazed beneath his bushy brows. "One of my chariots," he shouted, "is worth more than all your wooden-headed soldiers!"

"Please, please!" King Jabin exclaimed. "I said that we need to know more about the matter."

But Sisera was not to be silenced. "Prince Etzer may indeed be of the royal family," he cried, "but the strength of Canaan lies not in his army but in my chariots. Would all the tribes and peoples about us submit to our rule were it not for fear of my chariots?"

"Chariots, chariots!" Prince Etzer flung back. "One would think that Hazor and Canaan did not exist before you came along with that iron cart of yours!"

King Jabin rapped sharply on the table. "We must reach a decision in this matter," he snapped. "Commander Sisera, what is your position?"

"Forget Mount Tabor," Sisera responded, breathing heavily. "The mere sound of my chariot wheels will frighten the Israelite jackals away."

"And you believe otherwise?" the King turned to his cousin.

"I do indeed," the Prince replied. "When we first took up the matter I looked at it from the point of view of an army man, and I felt sure that victory for the Israelites would be impossible. But when I think back to the history of these tribes of Israel, I must look at it differently. By all the rules of war, they should never have been able to escape from Egypt, or survive forty years in the desert, or defeat Sihon and Og, or bring about the downfall of Jericho. Yet all this really took place."

"You mean that the Israelites might be aided by some kind of miracle?" one of the councillors asked.

"This I do not know," the Prince said. "What I do know is that every one of those miracles came only after the Israelites had made the first move to free themselves. At the Red Sea, they had to plunge into the water before the Sea opened before them. At Jericho, too, they laid a seven-day siege before the walls came down. I say, therefore, that if we allow the Israelites to take action by fortifying Mount Tabor, there may come another one of those miracles by their God, who may be as powerful as our noble chariots."

Sisera flung his whip down on the table. "And *I* say," he snarled, "that if a single Canaanite soldier is present at Mount Tabor I shall keep my chariots in their quarters, and let Hazor shift for itself as best it can!"

Prince Etzer looked at Sisera with unconcealed disgust. "The safety of Canaan does not mean as much to you as having your own way, Commander?"

Sisera turned to the King. "Sire," he cried, "are you going to do such a silly thing as having Mount Tabor fortified?"

King Jabin looked about him. This was a decision which he could not escape. All at once his round face brightened. Rarely did such a good idea come to him!

70

"We want to stop any Israelite uprising, yes," he declared. "We might be able to do this without fortifying Mount Tabor — at least for the present. I shall immediately issue an order that the Israelites are to use the country roads only. I shall also forbid them to travel in groups of more than ten people. Any movement on their part not in accordance with my orders will be punishable by death for all concerned." He looked about in triumph. "The meeting of the council is closed."

CHAPTER SIX

NEW DEVELOPMENTS

When Arnon awakened on what he felt sure would be his last day in Hazor, the sun was already shining brightly through the trees outside his window. He did not expect to meet with any difficulty in leaving Jabin's capital. Prince Etzer had promised him permission to visit Kedesh every once in a while. He would therefore casually take leave of the Prince and his household, then return to Barak and Deborah.

The seed had been sown. By the time that Barak and the men of Israel were ready to array their forces on Mount Tabor, the Canaanites would be ready to believe that they had a real revolt on their hands. Sisera and his chariots would be drawn into attacking the mountain, just as the Prophetess Deborah wanted.

Arnon glanced at the sun. His lesson with Nasik would take little more than an hour, but first he must seek out Prince Etzer and ask leave to visit Kedesh.

Then, just as he was about to call for Nasik, there came a message from Prince Etzer. Under no condition, said the message, was Arnon to leave the palace grounds unless and until permitted to do so by the Prince himself.

Arnon's heart sank. Now how would he be able to convey a message to his father? There was something else that Barak must be warned about, besides the council meeting: Heber the Kenite! For a moment Arnon thought of disobeying Prince Etzer's orders and trying to leave the town, without permission, but he realized that the palace guards might already have been told not to let him get away.

Only one course remained open: to speak to Prince Etzer himself. If it looked as if the order to remain in the palace would hold for some time, then a break from Hazor would have to be made.

But the Prince was not at the breakfast table.

"Some urgent matter of state," Princess Piria said, in answer to Arnon's questioning look. She kept her eyes steadfastly on him. "You do not look well this morning, Arnon," she remarked. "Perhaps you and Nasik will delay your morning lesson."

Nasik, busy with his wheat cakes and honey, jerked up his head. "I want to go riding!" he protested.

"Your mother is right," Arnon said gently. "My head feels heavy, and the canter of a horse may shake it right off my shoulders. But we can do wood carving, if you like."

"Good," Nasik agreed, turning again to his wheat cakes.

Princess Piria patted her son on the head. "You have eaten enough, young man. Now go to your room and wait there for Arnon."

Outside the breakfast room there was a small enclosed garden. No windows opened on it, though it was open to the sky; the only other entrance was from the breakfast room itself. Princess Piria led the way to the garden and motioned to Arnon to join her on one of the stone benches.

"I know that you have received Prince Etzer's message," she began. "Be not disturbed. He merely wishes to see that no harm should befall you."

"Harm?" repeated Arnon.

"Yes," the Princess replied. "When the Prince came here from the council meeting, he told me that you might be in danger. You see, Arnon, a man in my husband's position is bound to have enemies, and those who hate him also have no love for his family — or his friends."

"Sisera?" Arnon ventured.

Princess Piria nodded. "Yes, Sisera. I have no words to describe the hatred of that brute charioteer for my husband, and I fear it greatly." She sighed. "The thunder of Sisera's chariot wheels has cast a spell over our people. Everything that Sisera does is accepted without question. He would even attack the Philistines if the Prince did not stand in his way."

"The Philistines!" echoed Arnon in dismay. "Even Sisera's chariots cannot best them."

"True indeed," said the Princess. "But Sisera believes they can."

Arnon shook his head. "Prince Etzer must be in danger too, if Sisera is so powerful."

"Yes, he is," Princess Piria replied. "My only hope

is that King Jabin will not let himself be blinded by Sisera and his wild schemes." She rose from the bench. "I am sure that the Prince will want to see you as soon as he returns. In the meantime, Nasik is eagerly waiting." She placed her hand on Arnon's shoulder. "We all are so grateful to you, Arnon. Nasik was a very lonely boy before you came. I do hope that you and he will be together for a long time."

For the next hour Arnon and his pupil whittled away at their woodwork. Then, for good measure, the young teacher showed Nasik a few wrestling tricks. By noon both were ready for a bit of rest.

Arnon strolled out to the stables. Nehag was probably out with Prince Etzer, he thought. But as he rounded the corner of the stone building he saw to his surprise that the Prince's personal one-horse chariot was leaning, shaft up, against the wall.

The elderly stable-man was putting away fodder in the bins. "No, I haven't seen Nehag today," he replied curtly to Arnon's question.

"Do you know where he is?" Arnon persisted.

The stable-man shook his head, then gave the Israelite youth a quick glance. Finally his curiosity got the better of him. "Why are you looking for him?" he asked.

"Nehag has been overworking his tongue again," Arnon replied. "He has made a good deal of trouble for me."

"Is that so?" snorted the stable-boy. "Well, what did you expect? Did you think Nehag would keep your story to himself?"

"You are right," Arnon admitted. "I've already had to appear before the royal council because of it."

The stable-boy chuckled. "Everyone in Hazor knows about it," he said. "Even the children know what happened in the council chamber. Some of our councillors like to talk, and news becomes known as soon as they sit down in the first tavern."

Another stable-boy came in, just in time to overhear the conversation. "If I were you," he growled at his companion, "I wouldn't talk to this Israelite upstart. Nehag will break you in two."

Arnon laughed. "By the way," he remarked, "has Nehag ever told you men why he hates me?"

The stable-boys looked at each other. "I'd guess it's because you showed him up when you saved little Nasik in the runaway chariot," one of them said.

Arnon chuckled. "So Nehag never did tell you when and how we first met!"

"No, he never did," the other hand said.

Arnon briefly recounted the incident on the road to Ramah. "In a wrestling match Nehag would probably break me in two," he admitted, "but out on the highway, sprawled out on his back in the dust, he really looked foolish — and he knew it."

The stable-men regarded Arnon with new respect. "This is the first time that Nehag has been bested," the older man said, shaking his head. He took a deep breath. "For this you deserve to be told the whole story. Perhaps it will save you later on."

"I shall be grateful to you," Arnon said.

"The way we heard it," the man began, "Nehag

went to Prince Etzer with the story that you told us yesterday. The Prince, according to Nehag, didn't put much stock in it. Nehag then went to the head man of King Jabin's personal guard and told him the same story. Then Sisera learned about it, and that was when the King had you summoned to the council meeting."

"Tell him what happened afterwards," the other stable-boy urged.

"Don't hurry me; I shall," his companion said. "Late yesterday afternoon, after the council meeting, Prince Etzer drove off in his chariot. Shortly afterwards, Nehag disappeared. We couldn't find him anywhere."

Arnon whistled in surprise. "And he has been missing since?"

"Well, yes and no," the stable-boy replied. "Later that evening one of my friends who works in King Jabin's stables came here and asked me what Nehag was up to. It seems that he had been making the rounds of the taverns, boasting how he had uncovered an Israelite plot."

Arnon smiled to himself. Nehag was the last person in the world whom he would expect to help him spread his story in Hazor!

"Along with that," continued the stable-man, "Nehag began boasting about his own loyalty to Canaan. Then, as he drank more and more, he set about arousing the people against Prince Etzer because he had taken you into the palace."

Arnon bit his lip; this could mean trouble for the Prince. But the stable-man's next words did much to reassure him.

"Some of Nehag's friends dragged him out and took him somewhere to sleep off his drink. Prince Etzer is a favorite with the people of Hazor, and Nehag was just about ready to get himself into hot water. Anyway, he didn't come back last night. For all we know, he may never come back."

The conversation was suddenly interrupted by the clatter of hooves in the courtyard. Arnon and the stable-boy rushed out of the fodder bin just as a chariot came to a grinding halt in front of the door. At the reins, grim and tight-lipped, was Prince Etzer. Behind him, huddled in a heap on the floor of the chariot, lay Nehag.

The Prince sprang down to the ground and stood aside as Nehag, his eyes bloodshot and swollen, clambered down slowly.

"Get your things together and be gone at once," the Prince commanded. "If you are ever again seen in Hazor after today's sunset, I shall have you flogged."

Nehag turned away and tottered into the stable, muttering incoherently under his breath.

"Take care of the horse and the chariot," Prince Etzer ordered the stable-boys. "You, Arnon, come with me."

It was the first time that Arnon had been in Prince Etzer's private chamber. The large square room was fascinating for the youth to behold. Along two of the walls, neatly arrayed in tiers one above the other, were all the tools of war known to Arnon and a good many others which he now saw for the first time.

Bright javelins and heavy spears, swords of all shapes and sizes, plain shields and odd-shaped ones, daggers and battle hammers, slim bows and heavy archery, all these adorned the walls from floor to ceiling.

"Now, Arnon," began the Prince, taking off his riding helmet, "it is time that we talk about your future in Hazor." He gave the boy a searching look. "I haven't yet decided what to make of your story. This rumored Israelite plan to fortify Mount Tabor sounds just wild enough to have some truth to it." He drew a deep breath. "Under other circumstances I would have overlooked your part in relating the story to Nehag and the others, but I am afraid it is too late. Nehag has been spreading the tale in every tavern in Hazor, as I learned when I drove into town this morning. The people are in an ugly mood. Like Sisera, they are angry because the Israelites dare to even think of rising against Canaan. Therefore, much as the Princess and I — and, of course, Nasik — would like to have you stay here with us, your presence would be unwise. You will, therefore, select one of my best horses, which I shall give to you as a gift, and tonight you must leave Hazor forever."

"What about Sisera?" Arnon asked.

A puzzled frown came to Prince Etzer's face. "What do you mean, Arnon?"

"It will become known that I am gone, sir," Arnon answered. "Will not Sisera accuse you of letting me escape?"

The Prince laughed heartily, much to Arnon's relief. "Do not worry about Sisera," he remarked. "If he were to denounce me for your 'escape', as you call it, he would be admitting that there is truth to your story, which in turn means that your Israelites are not afraid of his chariots. This is a thought which I am sure Sisera cannot bear."

Arnon decided to ask a daring question. "What if the Israelites are indeed planning a revolt, sir?"

Prince Etzer looked steadfastly at the boy before him. "I am a Canaanite, Arnon. I intend to keep my people in power as long as I am alive. I intend to put down any effort to break our hold on what we have. But I also know that sooner or later all this will come to a test. That is the way of the affairs of men. One of these days, you Israelites will become inspired by that God of yours, and we Canaanites will have a battle on our hands."

Arnon made no attempt to hide his amazement. This Prince Etzer was a strange man! "What do you mean, sir, by our being inspired by our God?"

The Prince laughed kindly. "Perhaps you are too young to understand it, Arnon. When you go again to Ramah, be sure to ask the Prophetess about what I have just told you."

Again Arnon took a bold step. "Would you be angry, sir, if I were to ask you for the meaning of your words?"

"No, of course not," the Prince replied. "Yet I must warn you that these are my own thoughts. I share them with none of my friends at court. I am convinced that your people are now in our power only because they abandoned their God. Yes," he added, seeing the questioning look in Arnon's eyes, "today a change of heart may be taking place among your people, thanks to Deborah the Prophetess. She has been trying to renew the faith of the Israelites in their God, and that is why I think that she is a bigger threat to us than any man."

"Then our enslavement by the Canaanites is our punishment for having abandoned our God?" asked Arnon, as the Prince fell silent.

"You can call it that," Prince Etzer replied. "But let me explain it to you a little more clearly. You see, when your ancestors came into this land, under Joshua, all of Canaan trembled before their advance. Our fathers did put up some resistance, but knew that it would be useless to battle against your God. But, little by little, the Israelites began to take up our ways and to worship our Gods, up here in our territory and elsewhere. When we saw what was going on we could not believe our eyes, at first. Why should the Israelites abandon their powerful God and turn to ours -- unless their own mighty God had abandoned *them?* Do you follow my reasoning, Arnon?"

The boy nodded, but said nothing.

"We were no longer afraid," continued the Prince. "Without their God to help them and perform miracles for them, the Israelites were weak. Therefore, we Canaanites, and the Moabites and others, began to attack them — and we found that we were right. They yielded to our power as butter yields to the heat of the sun."

"But now?" asked Arnon. "Do you feel that the

Israelites are returning to their God ?"

Prince Etzer smiled. "You should know the answer to that," he replied, "had you ever listened to Deborah the Prophetess. Of course, we have our men moving about among your people, and they have been reporting the words of the Prophetess and her influence on the tribes of Israel. She says nothing that one may call dangerous, you understand, but her words of wisdom are very comforting — and comfort also lends strength." The Prince gave Arnon's shoulder a friendly squeeze. "Now that I have filled your ears with words, it is time that you prepare to leave."

It was a sad farewell that Arnon bade to the household of Prince Etzer, even though, for Nasik's sake, everyone pretended that the parting would be for a very short time. Arnon found himself wishing that these people were not Canaanites, the enemies of his people, and that, if victory were to crown the Israelite revolt, at least this household would be spared as Rahab's was when the walls of Jericho came down.

In the stable, Arnon selected a spirited black horse and led it through the darkened streets until he came to the main gate. Most of the walled towns in the land kept their gates closed during the night, but not in the Kingdom of Hazor. Sisera insisted that they remain open. No enemy, he declared, would dare to attack a Canaanite town at any time of the day or night — not with nine hundred iron chariots ready to strike back with swift and dreadful punishment !

The guards assigned to the gate were nowhere to be seen when Arnon, still leading his horse, came near. He could hear their voices off in a nearby tavern. Arnon wondered where Nehag was at that moment.

Once outside the town, the boy swung up onto the horse's back and set out at a gallop southward. There was something that he felt he had to clear up before returning to Kedesh. Otherwise it might be too late.

Heber the Kenite — just where did he stand?

Arnon's mind went over the words that Heber had spoken at the home of Deborah, less than two weeks earlier. Yes, the Kenites had reason to feel friendly toward the Israelites. After all, their clan was descended from Jethro, the father-in-law of Moses. But people tended to forget what had happened in the past. Right now King Jabin was more important to the Kenites than Jethro. Still, mused Arnon, Heber did not agree with the others of his clan; he had even moved his dwelling away from them.

Then Arnon recalled Prince Etzer's words...

He urged the horse forward. Elon-Bezaananim, or Elon, the place where Heber lived, was not too far away even in the dead of the night. Why not go directly to Heber's tent and try to seek out the truth?

Once or twice Arnon drew his mount into the shadows as a chariot clattered by. Finally, some distance away from Mount Tabor, he turned off the main highway. Being familiar with the road to Elon, he let the horse canter until he came to the outskirts of the village. Here he reined in. He had never been to Heber's tent, but there was something that would identify it. Since Heber dwelled apart from the rest, his tent would be some distance away.

Then he saw it, standing alone in the moonlight, pegged fast to the ground. Dismounting, he approached it cautiously, listening for any sound that came from within.

There was none. Arnon took a step closer. "Heber!" he called softly.

A slight rustle came to his ears. "Who speaks?" a woman's voice said.

"It is I, Arnon, son of Barak of Kedesh."

"What do you wish?"

"To speak with Heber."

"What is it that you wish to tell him?"

For a moment Arnon did not answer. He certainly could not tell Yael why he had come to Elon.

The tent flap slowly moved aside, and Yael stepped out into the darkness. Arnon caught the gleam of earrings in the moonlight, but otherwise her features were completely hidden in the folds of her hood.

"Speak, O son of Barak," she said softly, "though Heber is not here."

There was nothing else to do, then, thought Arnon, but to go to Kedesh.

"You do not come from the Prophetess," continued Yael.

"No, I do not," Arnon replied. "But how would you know that?"

"From Ramah did Heber come, with the girl," Yael replied.

"The girl?" echoed Arnon. "You mean Tirza?"

A slight smile came to Yael's lips at the change in Arnon's voice. "Your heart is with this girl," she said evenly. "You must pray to your God, for soon she will be in great danger. But tomorrow night you are all to be on Mount Tabor... while all is quiet, for the storm is brewing."

Arnon was taken aback. What could Yael possibly mean? Was Tirza going to be in danger because Heber was with her? And where had he taken her? Perhaps he was going to deliver her into the hands of the Canaanites! But then, surely Deborah would not have allowed Tirza to go with Heber if... Yes, the Prophetess trusted him, and that was enough.

Yael's voice broke in on the boy's thoughts. "Strange things will be going on in our midst very soon," she said. "But now, I shall give you food and drink, for you are weary and in need of rest."

Arnon followed Yael into the tent and sank to the ground. He was so tired that he ate the food which the Kenite woman placed before him almost without knowing what he was doing.

Then his eyes closed and he fell asleep.

CHAPTER SEVEN

IN SISERA'S CITY

Behind the wooded Carmel range, at the point where the Vale of Zevulun and the Vale of Jezreel come together, was Haroshet-Hagoyyim, the Iron City of Canaan.

A stranger would have hardly considered it to be in any way attractive, or even a comfortable place in which to live. A cloud of soot always hung above the city, and the sound of pounding hammers rang through its grimy streets from dawn till dark. The townspeople had to shout to make themselves heard; therefore, it was the custom in Canaan to say to him who spoke too grandly: "Go make yourself heard in Haroshet!"

And yet the grit-laden air and the ring of the anvils were the pride of the townspeople, even though the soot caused their eyes to smart and their throats to burn. No music sounded as sweet to their ears as did the clanging hammers, and they would not have exchanged the soot for the purest mountain air. For Haroshet-Hagoyyim, because it produced Commander

87

Sisera's chariots, *was* Canaan. Its heroes were the brawny, grime-encrusted men of the iron works. Day after day they toiled, fashioning new chariots for their master, the "iron man" of Canaan and the terror of the land from the Philistine border to Gilead. At night, when work was done, the smiths gathered in the taverns to recount their deeds and to bask in the admiration of the townspeople.

Sisera, himself, so it was said, had been a blacksmith's apprentice in his early youth, when Haroshet was no larger than an ordinary village. He was not yet full grown — so went the story — when he appeared before King Jabin's father. The King had only to give the word and he, Sisera the son of Gaava, would make Canaan so strong that it would be safe and secure forever.

"Even from the Israelites?" the elder Jabin had asked, recalling that Joshua had burned Hazor to the ground when the Israelites first entered the land.

"Especially from the Israelites," Sisera assured the Canaanite ruler.

"What is it that you plan, O young one?" the King wanted to know, "and how do you propose to do it?"

"Tomorrow," promised Sisera, "you shall have the answer."

On the very next day a strange contraption had come rolling into Hazor. Very little of it was visible to the curious onlookers. Its body, down to the wheels, was hidden by straw mats, tightly fastened at all points from front to rear. It was drawn by a single

88

horse, and the noise that it made as it rattled over the stones was like thunder. And many were those who swore that they saw sparks of fire beneath the straw mats.

In the inner courtyard of the royal palace, hidden from all except the King and his closest advisers, Sisera uncovered the strange vehicle. One by one the mats came off, and before the eyes of the bystanders there stood a chariot — and what a chariot! Such vehicles were already known, but this one, completely clad with iron, also had iron frames on all sides but the rear, to protect the archers and the spearmen. These frames could be swung open easily by means of a spring-and-socket device to allow the warriors to launch their own attack in the twinkling of an eye. The rear of the chariot had been left open because, as Sisera said, no enemy would ever see this Canaanite chariot in retreat.

The King and his advisers were impressed beyond words. Sisera was taken into the palace and showered with gifts. He then made a request, and it was immediately granted: his native town, Haroshet-Hagoyyim, was to be made the center of the chariot-building, and Sisera, crowned with the title of Commander, was to be its ruler.

The young blacksmith lost no time. Now that his word was law, the strongest men in the land were drafted to work in the smithies. Thousands toiled in the hills, mining the iron ore. Those who rebelled or faltered were shown no mercy.

As charioteers, Sisera chose the most daring and

fearless men in Canaan and from beyond its borders, for it soon became known that none lived better or enjoyed greater favors than did the drivers of Sisera's iron chariots.

The Commander lost none of his influence when young Jabin came to the throne. Already his chariots had frightened the Israelites into submission. The surrounding countries were most eager to be on good terms with Hazor, and Canaan was soon enjoying such prosperous days as no one could recall. Taxes and gifts poured into the royal treasury like swollen streams of water in Spring, and the splendor of the palace was the envy of kings and chieftains far and wide.

Sisera, not content with all this, wanted to spread the power of his chariots beyond the Lebanon and the Sea of Salt. But one man stood in his way. Since King Jabin had no children, the next in line to the throne was his cousin, Prince Etzer — and the Prince would not let Sisera have his own way. Canaan was already at the height of its power, he pointed out, without having had to conquer the surrounding territories; why make enemies of them? And certainly there was already enough wealth in the land, even to take care of the high-living charioteers.

Sisera's fury knew no bounds. He thundered and threatened. He shouted that the days of the foot-soldier were gone — a strong statement, seeing that Prince Etzer was the commander of the Canaanite army.

Poor King Jabin was caught in the middle. He tried

to keep Sisera happy by arranging races and tournaments for his charioteers, with rich prizes for the winners. But the former blacksmith's apprentice was not to be appeased. And many were the townspeople who said that if Prince Etzer would ever come to the throne, Sisera would remove him from it.

Sisera's feelings toward Prince Etzer were shared by every man, woman and child in Haroshet-Hagoyyim, but none hated the Prince more than did Gaava, Sisera's mother, who ruled the Commander's household with such an iron hand that Sisera himself had never married, in fear that any wife he might take would displease his mother.

Before her son rose to power, Gaava lived in a humble hut and worked in the fields. Now, comfortably settled in a large wing of Sisera's palace (the personal gift of King Jabin), she passed the time cursing Prince Etzer, praising her son, and fingering the fine ornaments Sisera sent her after every tax collection.

Yet even in the ointment of Gaava's life there was a troublesome fly. So ill-tempered was she that none of her maids would stay with her very long, and Sisera warned his mother not to take strong measures against them; Canaanite girls were proud. The dutiful son solved the problem by replacing the native maids with slave girls from other territories. With these Gaava could do as she pleased. They were forbidden to leave the palace grounds. One or two tried to escape; the whip of Makke, keeper of the palace dungeon, soon put a stop to such attempts.

Except when he was away on some expedition, Sisera came to see his mother every day. His visits were brief, however, since he liked nothing better than to work in his private smithy, built on the palace grounds.

The Canaanite warrior was pounding away at a brace which he had designed when one of the guards entered. Someone was asking to speak to the Commander about a most important matter.

It was Nehag whom Sisera's sentry ushered in.

The charioteer looked even worse than he had when Prince Etzer sent him packing from Hazor. He had made the journey to Haroshet-Hagoyyim astride an ill-tempered mule he had conveniently "borrowed." An hour's distance from the city, the animal suddenly bolted, leaving the furious charioteer to make the rest of the way on foot.

Sisera recognized him at once, despite the dust that caked his face.

"What is your business here?" he demanded roughly. "Is your master with you?"

"Prince Etzer is no longer my master. May Baal strike him dead," Nehag replied. "I am here to seek a place among your charioteers."

Sisera gave him a long look. "Come with me," he said finally, leading the way back into the smithy. He leaned against the anvil and folded his arms across his hairy chest. "Now speak," he ordered, "and take care what you say."

Nehag wet his lips. "The Prince sent me away because I was telling people how he was favoring the

Israelite trouble-maker."

"Indeed!" Sisera's bushy eyebrows came together. "What do you mean, 'favoring'?"

"Judge for yourself, O Commander," exclaimed the charioteer. "When that foolish pup let slip that the Israelites were planning to fortify Mount Tabor, I lost no time telling the Prince about it. But do you know what he said to me? 'Dismiss it from your mind'—that is what he said." Nehag's voice rose shrilly. "There I was, a most loyal son of Canaan with news of a plot against my country, and noble Prince Etzer tells me to forget it!"

"And you therefore went to the King with the story?"

Nehag drew himself up. "Of course! I am a most loyal son of Canaan, by Baal! I also have friends among the King's advisers who know that I am loyal."

"Yes, yes, I know," Sisera interrupted sharply. "You are also a fool. You stirred up a storm over nothing at all. The Israelite was merely boasting."

The charioteer shook his head violently. "I swear he was telling the truth, Commander. You should have seen how frightened he became when he realized what he had said."

Sisera spat into the black dust. "Again I say that you are a fool, Nehag. The Israelites will never dare so much as wiggle a finger. They know that my chariots will crush their bones. As for your former employer, he too is a fool. He wants to fortify Mount Tabor just so that his foot soldiers will have something to do."

Nehag snickered, but his heart was far from merry. He had expected Sisera to welcome him with open arms. "This is only part of Prince Etzer's plan," he said, lowering his voice.

"So?" demanded Sisera. "What else has he in mind?"

"This I have been told by one of the servants," lied the charioteer. "He heard the Prince tell it to Princess Piria. The Prince is going to King Jabin with the demand that the money spent on maintaining your charioteers be cut down. He says that they are not worth it."

Rage mounted in Sisera's face so swiftly that for a moment he could not speak. Silently the charioteer congratulated himself on having thought of exactly the right thing, and just in time.

Sisera moved away from the anvil. "Over there," he said curtly, pointing to a long low building on the other side of the courtyard, "you will find Maslif, the chief of my charioteers. Give him my orders to provide you with clothes and quarters. If I want to talk to you later, I shall let you know." He turned sharply and stalked off, gritting his teeth. So Prince Etzer was finally moving against him, Commander Sisera! This was something that his mother would want to know.

At the entrance to Gaava's dwelling Sisera beheld the guard deep in argument with a stranger. The stranger turned around at the sound of Sisera's heavy footsteps.

"Ah, Commander Sisera!" he exclaimed with delight. "Baal be praised for your timely arrival! I was

95

about to lose patience with this unreasonable dullard who thinks he deserves to be your palace guard."

Sisera frowned. He had seen the stranger before. Then he remembered, and the flush on his face deepened. Heber the Kenite, of whom Prince Etzer had spoken so glowingly!

"How is your health, Commander?" continued Heber cheerfully. "It is some time since I sold you horses for your chariots — at a very low price, you will recall."

"Yes, I recall that great event," rasped Sisera impatiently. "Have you more horses — better ones, perhaps?"

Heber's face twisted in protest. "Better horses, Commander? None such exist, I assure you. Yet it is not as a trader of horses that I am here today, O most noble Sisera. No indeed. This time I am here because of your wonderful mother, may Baal bless her days, make her nights peaceful, her years long."

The frown on Sisera's face softened somewhat. "What is it that you have for my mother, O Kenite?"

Heber waved his hand grandly. "Ah, what if not the best?" he exclaimed. "Hear me, then! A few days ago I found myself near Taanach to collect payment for some wool that I had sold — not *my* wool, you understand, for who am I to own enough sheep to make shearing worthwhile? Now the man to whom I had sold this wool — he who lives near Taanach — *now* dares tell me that he has naught with which to pay for it. What does one do in a situation such as this, I ask you?"

"One talks less," retorted Sisera.

"Ah, yes, so one can," sighed Heber, "especially with this numbskull from Taanach. In the end he offers me not money but his daughter! 'Come,' I say to him. 'Why not marry her off to some young man who will pay you well for her, and you may then pay me for the wool?' And this man from Taanach looks at me and says: 'How can I marry her off when no one seeks her hand? For it is known that I come from a lowly family.' And such a girl, O Sisera, he wants to give me instead of money!"

"You have something for my mother?" demanded Sisera, now thoroughly irritated.

"This man from Taanach shows me his daughter, and I find her to be a comely maid. Then, as though Baal himself had sent the thought to my mind, I say to myself: 'Here indeed is a maiden fit to serve the most noble Gaava!' And indeed, O Sisera, cast your eyes upon her and see for yourself."

Sisera followed the sweep of the Kenite's arm to a tree that stood near the doorway. In its shade, wrapped in a light gray cloak, sat the girl, her eyes staring into the distance.

The Canaanite commander took a step toward the tree, then stopped. If the girl should happen to please Gaava, good enough. "Your gift is welcome," he said to Heber. "The guard will show her to her quarters." He grasped the Kenite by the arm and drew him away. "You have had dealings with Prince Etzer?" he demanded.

Heber nodded. "Several times have I had the honor,"

he replied lightly. "When, together with my fellow Kenites, I came to Hazor to assure King Jabin of our friendship, Prince Etzer received us most kindly. I also sold him several fine horses — not as fine as..."

"Enough, enough," interrupted Sisera. "You have more horses, O Kenite?"

"Good ones are becoming more and more difficult to obtain," sighed Heber, "yet I know that some may be had across the Jordan. How about blankets? Horses are like people, you know; they must be kept warm on cold nights. I must obtain blankets for Prince Etzer anyway."

Sisera's annoyance grew. "Talk not in riddles, fellow!" he exclaimed. "What is this about blankets for horses and Prince Etzer? What are you blabbing?"

Heber shrugged. "I think only as I hear," he replied. "Only today I heard, from merchants traveling along the highway, that Prince Etzer is planning to build a rest camp for his troops on Mount Tabor. Now even a child knows that the nights on Mount Tabor are cold, and therefore blankets will be needed. Why should I not be the one to provide them? One has to make a living."

As he was talking, Heber noticed that Sisera's face was turning purple.

"How many horses would you need?" the Kenite went on blandly.

The question helped Sisera regain control of himself. "Ten for the present, and in three days," he said curtly. "Now be gone with you." He turned away and disappeared into his smithy.

Heber cast a glance at the doorway into which Tirza had followed the guard, and prepared to leave the courtyard. He now reviewed the situation: Arnon was in Hazor, prodding the royal court into believing that an Israelite revolt was brewing; Tirza was now established in Gaava's household to feed the fires of hatred for Prince Etzer; and now Sisera believed that the Prince was determined to get his soldiers up on Mount Tabor one way or another.

The Kenite crossed the courtyard to the spot by the gate where he had left his own horse and Tirza's mule. As he passed by the barracks of Sisera's charioteers, he threw an idle glance in that direction and almost stopped in his tracks. There, strutting in front of the building in a new uniform, was the charioteer whom Arnon had bested on the road to Ramah.

Heber hurried on. What was Prince Etzer's personal driver doing in Haroshet-Hagoyyim? And had something happened to Arnon?

CHAPTER EIGHT

THE MEETING ON THE MOUNTAIN

It was almost noon when Arnon, riding at a steady canter, reached the outskirts of Ramah.

He had intended to stay on the main highway up to the point where the side road branched off to Deborah's home, but the deserted look of the town, even from a distance, made him stop short.

A shrill whistle from a clump of bushes by the highway came to his ears, and a moment later a small boy came running toward him.

"You on your way to the Prophetess?" the boy called up to Arnon. "Do not go. The Canaanites are there. Go to the inn." He disappeared into the bushes as suddenly as he had come.

Arnon urged his horse toward the town. Here again was something strange, but the events of the past two weeks had taught him not to try to understand everything.

He found the innkeeper in the courtyard, whittling away at a rough plank. At the sound of the hoofbeats the man looked up, laid aside his work and motioned to Arnon to follow him inside the house.

The dining hall was empty. The innkeeper nodded toward a stool at the table. "Be seated, son of Barak."

Arnon lost no time. "A boy on the road told me about Canaanites in the house of the Prophetess and that I was to come here. What means all this?"

"That was one of my sons," the innkeeper told him. "Another is up the road, above the house. We want no one to enter Ramah."

"But the Canaanites," persisted Arnon, "what are they doing in Deborah's house?"

The innkeeper chuckled. "No harm has befallen the Prophetess. As for our noble masters, they are in Deborah's house because she so planned it. Before daybreak yesterday she had a message placed by an 'Israelite traitor,' on the doorstep of the Canaanite barracks up the hill, saying that with nightfall there will be a gathering in her house to plot an uprising against King Jabin."

Arnon's breath came a little faster.

"The Canaanite soldiers," continued the innkeeper, "waited until dark, then swooped down like a pack of hungry wolves. Of course, they found the house empty. This caused some confusion, as the Prophetess had said they would be there. Was there really a plot, or was the message some sort of prank? Should the matter be reported to Hazor? If so, who and where were the plotters, and why were they allowed to escape?"

"What did they finally do?" asked Arnon.

"Exactly what Deborah said they would do. One of

our men, perched high in a tree inside the wall, heard the Canaanites decide to send a chariot to Hazor to report the whole matter as a rumor, and at the same time to leave four of themselves inside the house, just in case the 'plotters' returned."

"But you say that the Prophetess is safe?" inquired Arnon anxiously. "Will not the Canaanites seek her out?"

Again the innkeeper chuckled. "They have come here, and elsewhere in Ramah, asking for her whereabouts, whereupon they were told that she had gone north, to judge the people in the Kedesh area."

The mention of Kedesh stirred Arnon's memory. "How did you know who I am?" he asked the innkeeper.

"The Prophetess sent word that you would be along," was the reply. "Besides, I remember when you first came here with your grandfather. You did not sleep too much that night, eh?"

The question caused Arnon's mind to flash to Tirza, and, despite himself, his face reddened.

"Had you arrived here yesterday," the innkeeper went on, "I would have told you to keep going to Kedesh. Today you are to wait here until the afternoon, then go on to Mount Tabor, but you are to proceed carefully." He paused at the startled look that came into Arnon's eyes. "What is wrong?" he demanded.

"That is exactly what Yael told me to do!" Arnon exclaimed.

"You mean that Kenite woman?" The innkeeper

drew a deep breath. "She is a strange one. There are many who are afraid of her." He rose and headed back to the courtyard. "You may rest or do whatever you like here," he said to Arnon, "but be sure to be on your way before dark."

The sun was still three hours away from the western horizon when Arnon led his horse out of the courtyard. The hours had dragged by slowly, even though the youth had insisted on helping the innkeeper with his work. But this was no time for impatience. Every step had to be taken exactly as planned.

Arnon followed a side road that wound between the hills and opened into the plain around Mount Tabor. By the time that he reached the plain, only the stars could be seen in the darkness.

Arnon's horse came to a halt at the edge of a break in the ground. This was the Kishon, a stream that wound from the foot of Tabor and flowed through the vale of Zevulun into the Great Sea. As always in late Spring, the bed of the stream was dry. Arnon urged his mount down the bank and up the other side.

Like his friends, Arnon knew every inch of the ground; there was no better spot in the land south of the Galilee itself, for camping and hiking. Still, since Deborah as well as Yael had ordered him to take care, he would have to proceed as though he had never been in the vicinity of Tabor at all.

Arnon tied his horse to a tree at the foot of the mountain. He scanned the heavens above him. Yael had said that clouds would be gathering at Tabor's crest, but not a wisp could be seen between the darkness that crowned it and the stars overhead.

Tightening his sandal-straps, Arnon went on to one of the trails that led up the uneven slope, ducking under the branches that extended across the rocky path. At each bend of the trail, mindful of Yael's warning, he paused to listen.

A good two hundred paces up the mountain, there was a clearing large enough to hold many hundreds of campers. Arnon decided to skirt the area, just in case anyone happened to be about.

He was still a good hundred paces away from the spot when his ears caught the murmur of voices. Another few steps forward and Arnon stopped short; there was no mistaking the voice of the speaker, for that was how Barak talked whenever he addressed the people of Kedesh.

Arnon was about to straighten up and head for the clearing when his eyes, now thoroughly accustomed to the darkness, caught sight of a slight movement a few paces to his left. He saw the top of a bush sway back and forth, followed by a hardly audible scraping sound.

It might have been an animal, but for some reason Arnon felt sure that it was not anything four-legged. He remained listening as the scraping sound moved higher upward, toward the clearing.

The creeping prowler was now in Arnon's full view. The figure he beheld was without doubt that of a man, dressed in black and hugging the ground as he kept wriggling forward.

Arnon thought quickly. He could shout to the men

above and try blocking the prowler, or he could attempt to pin him down where he lay. He decided to do both. Crouched slightly, he pressed his foot into the earth for a better foothold and crashed up the slope toward the man on the ground, shouting as he charged.

He almost missed his quarry. At the first sound of Arnon's voice the prowler rolled over quickly and in the same motion rose to his feet. Another step and he would have escaped Arnon's lunge entirely. As it was, Arnon barely managed to catch hold of the stranger's ankle and hang on to it. Then the prowler's other foot caught him in the temple, and suddenly Mount Tabor began to flash with shooting stars.

When Arnon recovered his senses he found himself lying on the grass. Squatting by his side were two men. One of them was bending over him, and Arnon recognized the rugged features of Nissan.

The "camel driver" raised a finger to his lips. But Arnon was too astonished to utter a sound, for now he could see the black-garbed prowler as he sat on the ground, with Barak towering above him.

Arnon looked again in disbelief. No, he was not mistaken. The prowler was Prince Etzer!

Nissan gently pushed the boy back. It would not do to let the Prince see who it was that had captured him.

"Prince Etzer," Arnon heard Barak say, "I do not know how much you have overheard, but there are two things that you now know very well. You know that we are plotting against the rule of your kinsman, King Jabin, and against Canaan. You must also be aware that we cannot allow you to return to Hazor."

"Your reasoning is such that I find no fault with it," the Prince commented drily. "I am obviously in your power."

Barak drew a deep breath. "I take it, Prince, that someone has informed you of our plan to fortify Mount Tabor. We have tried to keep it a secret."

"Indeed?" There was a touch of irony in Prince Etzer's tone. "And here I was beginning to think that you were making every effort to have all Canaan learn about it." He laughed harshly. "Whoever that young man was whom you managed to get into my household, he surely created enough confusion to set Hazor seething with rumors. But I still think that you Israelites are very foolish. Even if you do succeed in fortifying Mount Tabor, it will be an easy matter for Sisera and his chariots to surround the mountain and starve you to death."

Barak shrugged. "If you, Prince EEtzer, were the commander of the charioteers, perhaps what you say would be true. But we know Sisera. And who can tell? Perhaps Sisera may yet believe that it is you and your foot-soldiers who are encamped on Tabor. He hates you, Prince Etzer, and he is afraid of you. What if he takes it into his head to storm Tabor, knowing that you and your men are there, and then pretending that he thought it was the Israelites whom he had attacked? What say you to that?"

Arnon waited for Prince Etzer's answer, but the Canaanite nobleman did not reply right away. When he spoke, his voice showed no trace of emotion.

"What do you intend to do with me?" he asked evenly. "My absence will soon be noticed, and I assure you that King Jabin will have the land searched as with a fine comb if I do not return."

Barak spread his hands. "What choice do we have?" he exclaimed. "Can we allow you to go back to Hazor and put our plans to naught? No, we have suffered the Canaanite yoke long enough and none will stand in the way of our struggle for freedom. Yet, with the consent of my comrades, I am prepared to let you go."

A grunt of surprise came from the thirty-odd men gathered about Barak.

"Yes, you will be allowed to return to Hazor," continued the Israelite leader, "if you give us your word that you will neither reveal our plans nor take any part in hindering them."

Prince Etzer stiffened. "You are talking to the commander of the Canaanite army, sir," he cried. "What you are proposing is an insult!"

"Take it as you wish," Barak returned. "Yet let us look again at the matter. Do you believe that our revolt may succeed?"

"Never," snapped the Prince. "It is the dream of a child!"

"Then why spurn my offer?" urged Barak. "Even if you take no hand in the fighting you will not endanger Hazor since, as you say, victory for us is impossible."

For a moment Prince Etzer appeared to be wrestling with himself. "I accept your offer, but you are all madmen. Your cause is doomed to defeat. You simply cannot win."

Barak shook his head. "You are wrong, Prince. We *can* win — because we *must!* Another generation under Canaanite rule and our people will lose even the will to fight for their freedom. Then we shall cease to be a people, as our ancestors would have done in Egypt. Fortunately Moses came in time, and fortunately the God of our fathers sent us a Moses."

Prince Etzer chuckled. *"You* do not seem possessed of the modesty with which I believe your great leader was blessed."

It was Barak's turn to laugh, as did the men about him. "I wished to spare you this," he replied, "but in my own defense I must say that the defeat of Canaan will come at the hands of a woman."

"Deborah the Prophetess!" exclaimed the Prince softly.

"Indeed you have guessed the truth," Barak replied. "Now, do we have your word?"

"You have," the Prince replied shortly. "I give you my word not to reveal your plans nor to hinder them. But once your foolish revolt breaks out, I shall consider myself free to do whatever I wish."

"Let it be as you say," agreed Barak. "You may now depart."

Prince Etzer rose and glanced at the silent circle around him. They were all strangers to him, these sober-faced men, his enemies — just as he was theirs. Yet they were prepared to stake their entire future, their very lives, on his word of honor. Why?

Barak sensed what was in Prince Etzer's mind. "We know you, Prince Etzer," he said slowly. "Were you the ruler of Hazor, perhaps it would not be necessary for us to be here, for among the Canaanites we know you as a just man, a man of reason. We therefore believe in your word." His voice softened. "Perhaps when peace descends on this land we shall yet meet in friendship."

The Prince turned quickly and headed down the main trail. A moment later his footsteps could no longer be heard.

As one, the men in the clearing surrounded Arnon, patting him lustily on the back.

"A most unusual lad!" exclaimed Nissan. "First he saves Prince Etzer's son, then he turns around and captures the father. And who knows what he has done in between!"

Barak helped his son to his feet, for Arnon was so embarassed that he could have crawled under the grass. "Do not make much of him, men," he said curtly — but there was no hiding the pride in his voice.

Nissan pretended to be outraged. "Will you not admit, O Barak," he demanded, "that your son's capture of the Prince may mean the difference between victory and defeat?"

But Barak had little time for pleasantries. He ordered his men into the center of the clearing, away from the wooded rim of the slope.

Arnon managed to keep himself and Nissan a bit behind the others. "Why was Prince Etzer allowed to go free?" he asked in a whisper. "I know that he is a man of honor, yet..."

"Hah, yours is a sharp young mind," returned Nissan. "I, too, did not understand Barak's purpose immediately. Yet it is clear that the Prince's disappearance would only hinder our plans. For one, Sisera would, no doubt, be so pleased that he would be in no mood to accept our challenge at Tabor. And accept it he must, or everything will be lost. He and his chariots must be destroyed, if our hope of lifting the Canaanite yoke is to come to pass."

"And you do not think that Prince Etzer will try to warn Sisera?"

"Not directly, for he has given his word to us. But if he does try to discourage Sisera in any other way Sisera will readily believe that the Prince's real aim is to belittle him and his charioteers."

Arnon nodded in the darkness. "You are right. I heard enough in Hazor about Sisera's hatred for the Prince to last a lifetime."

Nissan gave him a playful nudge. "But otherwise your stay was enjoyable, you scamp."

Arnon was about to reply when his companion laid a warning hand on his arm. From some point below the clearing came the howling of a jackal — three long, mournful tones, then a fourth, a sharp one.

"Heber has arrived," Nissan grunted.

Arnon's heart beat faster. At last he would find out about Tirza; perhaps she was with him now!

But the Kenite, as he noiselessly emerged from the shadows, was alone. He headed straight for the clump of men. "Someone drove off in a chariot as I reached the bottom of the slope," he said anxiously. "Who was it?"

"Why not venture a guess?" suggested Nissan. "Since it was a chariot, the driver could not have been one of us."

Heber shook his head. "Who it was cannot be as important as why he was here. But as long as you know about him, I shall make no guesses."

"It was Prince Etzer," Barak informed the Kenite. "Arnon here had the good fortune to come upon him and make his capture possible, as he was lying there listening to our plans."

Heber whistled softly. "Prince Etzer, eh? This is remarkable. Only several hours ago I saw his personal charioteer in Haroshet-Hagoyyim, dressed in the uniform of Sisera's men." He turned to Arnon. "You remember him well, do you not?"

"Nehag? Very well," Arnon replied. "I also know that Prince Etzer had sent him away just before I left Hazor, with the threat that he would be flogged if he ever showed his face there again."

"Excellent!" cried Barak. "This means that this charioteer will further arouse Sisera's wrath. What else, Heber?"

"I am to bring to Sisera ten horses, three days from now. When are you bringing the men up here?"

The knot of men around the Kenite tightened. The hour of battle was drawing near.

"On the fourth night," answered Barak. "Sisera must not attack before the fifth day, past dawn. Thus did the Prophetess say."

CHAPTER NINE

TIRZA'S ADVENTURE

The large, almost shapeless woman lying on the soft cushions appeared to be asleep. Her blue-streaked eyelids were closed and no movement disturbed her heavy features. But every now and then her plump arm went groping toward the tray of sweets at her side, making the bracelets at her wrists tinkle lazily, and then the sound of slow chewing filled the chamber.

This was Gaava, mother of Commander Sisera and the terror of all maids in the palace. No matter what bothered Gaava — a cold gust of wind sweeping through the chamber, the sudden bark of a dog outside, a shriveled grape in the cluster on the tray — one of the maids was surely to blame. Hardly a day would go by without some unfortunate girl being dragged to the dungeon for a lashing.

Tirza learned all about Gaava even before the guard brought her to the maids' quarters, and so the Israelite girl was prepared. The very first time that she was summoned to wait on Sisera's mother, Tirza managed

to make known to Gaava her own "dislike" of Prince
Etzer and, on the other hand, her unbounded admiration of Commander Sisera and his charioteers.

Gaava was so delighted with her new maid that
Tirza immediately became her personal attendant. On
the very first day, she even allowed Tirza a most
unusual privilege — to enter the Treasure Chamber
all by herself. This small square room was next to
Gaava's own; its door was always kept locked and
Gaava alone had the key, right under her pillow.

The Treasure Chamber had but one window, a wide
opening some three hand's breadth in height, from
which one could look out on the entire palace courtyard. Whenever the trumpeter outside announced
Sisera's return from one of his journeys, Gaava would
hurry to this window, climb the squat stool beneath
it, and watch the chariots roll into the yard, often
laden with finery to add to her treasures. On the following day she would invite the highly-placed women
of Haroshet-Hagoyyim for a look at the new finery.
They all came — for none dared refuse the mother of
the Commander — and those who had known Gaava
when she lived in a mud hut left the palace sick with
envy.

Gaava took such a liking to the new "maid from
Taanach" that she placed her in charge of the Treasure Chamber. Tirza's heart skipped a beat when she
recognized, on top of the pile of finery, the beautiful
wares that the Canaanites had taken from the Ramah
Spring Market.

On the day set for Heber's return with the horses,

Tirza found the other maids in a state of buzzing excitement. From the gatekeepers they had learned that the Commander's nephew was about to arrive for a visit. The young man, an officer in the Canaanite army, was said to be very handsome and his grandmother's favorite as well.

To this excited chatter, Tirza paid little attention. Her mind was on Heber's expected visit and on how she could manage to talk to him. For there was something of great importance she had overheard Sisera tell his mother that morning: he, Sisera, the hero and savior of Canaan, was planning to go to Hazor and demand of King Jabin that the armed forces of the land — chariots and foot soldiers alike — be placed under one command — his own.

The hour was a little past noon, when Tirza usually went to the market place for a fresh supply of the sweets that Gaava loved so much. She picked up her basket and was about to enter Gaava's chamber for last-minute instructions, when the clatter of chariot wheels came from the inner courtyard.

"Ah, that must be my little Toar," Tirza heard her mistress exclaim. The next moment Gaava came bustling into the corridor. At the sight of Tirza she paused. "Wait before you go, my dear," she said. "You have not seen my Toar. You will be enslaved by his charm, by Baal!"

Tirza watched Gaava waddle off toward the doorway. This Toar might indeed be the handsomest man in the land, but there were more important matters to worry about. Toar would have to wait.

Then, without knowing why she did so, Tirza slipped into Gaava's room and took the key to the Treasure Chamber from under the pillow. Unlocking the door, she quickly replaced the key and left the room just as Gaava, cackling with laughter, came up the corridor.

"Just let me show her to you, Toar. A slave girl, yet so beautiful to look at—and a good attendant, by Baal!"

"It will be my pleasure to meet this beauty of yours," Tirza heard a man's voice reply. "You know that I do not run away from fair maidens."

Tirza thought her heart would stop. The voice had an all too familiar ring. An instant later she was looking into the eyes of Gaava's grandson.

He was the captain of the Ramah guards!

Although she managed to keep her own face calm, Tirza could see that Toar had recognized her at once.

"Aha! What did I tell you!" exclaimed Gaava in triumph, noting her grandson's sagging jaw. "A real beauty, is she not? But you shall see more of her later." She pushed Toar playfully but firmly into her own room. "Right now you must tell your old grandmother all about the adventures you have been having." She turned back to Tirza. "Come back quickly, girl," she said with a wink, "as I am sure you will."

Tirza waited until the curtain across the doorway stopped moving, then she quietly opened the door of the Treasure Chamber and slipped inside. It would take but a moment for Toar to recover from his surprise and tell his grandmother who her favorite servant really was.

The Chamber was almost dark, with only a thin shaft of light coming through the slit in the window curtains. The light cut through the room like a thin sword and came to rest on a pile of precious stones gleaming dully in their glazed earthenware boxes.

Tirza tried to picture to herself what was likely to happen. Toar might head for the market place, or he might go straight to Sisera and tell him about his having seen her in Deborah's home. She thought hard, — yes, he would go to the market place in the hope of bringing her back to Sisera himself, and thus appear more of a hero in his uncle's eyes. But since he would not find her in the market place, he would be forced to go to his uncle. What would Sisera be likely to do then? Would he send his charioteers to scour the countryside for her?

Heber! Tirza's heart beat faster. The Kenite was due to arrive with the horses before sunset. Unaware of what was taking place, he would head straight for his doom, unless Toar could somehow be kept from speaking to Sisera.

She pressed her ear to the wall that separated the Treasure Chamber from Gaava's room, but the wall was too thick. Tirza moved to the door. "Help me, O God of Deborah," she whispered — and opened the door a hand's breadth.

Gaava's plaintive voice came through the curtain. "Are you leaving me so soon, Toar? Or are you hurrying to the market place, to catch up with the pretty servant girl?"

"I shall catch up with her, never fear !" Toar replied, and Tirza could hear the fury in his voice. "Then I shall take her to the Commander."

The sound of many hooves came through the window behind the girl. Heber had arrived with the horses.

Tirza closed the door and hurried back. There, before Sisera's smithy, half a score of horses stood pawing the gritty earth.

She tried to make out the features of the man holding the reins. He did not look at all like Heber, yet his face was familiar. Could it be Arnon ? Tirza felt a warm flush mounting to her cheeks. Then she recognized the man, for Nissan had come several times with Barak to the home of the Prophetess.

But where was Heber ?

As if in answer, the Kenite came out of the smithy with Sisera at his side, swinging his whip. From Heber's gestures Tirza understood that the "horse dealer" was praising his steeds to the skies.

"Make them leave soon, O God !" Tirza prayed. The market place was just beyond the palace walls and, with few people about at this hour, it would not take Toar long to see that his quarry was not among them.

What caused the girl even greater worry was that Sisera was in no hurry. He went over each horse carefully from mane to tail, paying no attention to the constant chatter that came from Heber's lips. He did not pause even when he saw Toar approaching.

"I want to have word with you, my uncle," the

young officer said tersely.

"Hah! Greetings, Toar," Sisera answered. "What think you of these animals?"

Heber raised his arms to heaven. (Tears came to Tirza's eyes. What a man, that Heber! He, too, must have recognized Toar, and knew what it meant, but he was playing the game to the end.) "What ill can anyone say of such remarkable steeds?" he exclaimed. Not even Nissan could detect the slightest change in the Kenite's tone. "I assure you, Commander, that if you were to harness your chariots to lgihtning itself, you could not outstrip these beauties!"

Toar grasped Sisera's shoulder. "What is that Israelite girl doing in your mother's chamber?"

A startled frown covered Sisera's bearded face. "What has happened?" he demanded.

Heber burst into laughter. "It must be the one I brought from Taanach as a gift to the noble Gaava," he said easily. "Can it be that our young man here has lost his heart to her? Or," and his voice changed, "has she displeased her most worthy mistress?"

"From Taanach, eh?" retorted Toar, glaring at Heber. He turned to his uncle. "She comes from Ramah, and she is of the household of Deborah the Prophetess! I myself have seen her there."

Heber recoiled, as if struck by an unseen hand. "My dear young man," he cried, "you must indeed be mistaken. If the one you speak of is the one I brought, then indeed she comes from Taanach." A new thought appeared to have struck him. "Perhaps she has a twin sister, although the man from Taanach, her father..."

120

"Toar, are you sure that she is the girl you saw in the household of the Prophetess?" Sisera said slowly. His eyes never left Heber's face.

"May Baal strike me dead here in front of you, if what I say is not true," Toar cried. "I looked at her hard enough. Why, that brazen wench had the gall to refuse me..."

"Enough!" exclaimed Sisera. "I must know what she is doing here. You, Toar, call the guards. I want this Kenite and his companion thrown into the dungeon."

"I swear she comes from Taanach," Heber cried. "She may have been in someone else's house first but, by Baal, it was in Taanach that I saw her."

His protests were in vain. In another moment he and Nissan found themselves in the firm grip of the Commander's burly guards.

"To the dungeon," ordered Sisera. "I am on my way to Hazor. When I return, I shall question the pair of you. You, Toar, find the girl and keep watch over her until I come back."

Tirza stood trembling at the window. The worst had come to pass. Now everything was lost!

She tried to calm herself, to think of something. Toar, she knew, would leave no stone unturned to find her; he would like nothing better than revenge for the slight she had given him in refusing his invitation.

The rattle of chariot wheels came from the courtyard. Toar was off to look for her. When it was dusk he would come back to the palace. What then? How long could she remain in the Treasure Chamber?

This last thought quieted her. At least she would be safe where she was, with time to think. Gaava would be in no mood to pay a visit to her finery.

Tirza heard footsteps down the corridor and the sound of gruff voices. Heber and Nissan were being taken to the dungeon. Then the sounds died away.

The sound of a gong came faintly through the heavy door, once, twice... once, twice. Gaava was calling for her! She should have been back from the market place long ago. Again the gong sounded, this time loudly. Gaava was accustomed to an immediate response from her slave girls.

Tirza crouched behind a high pile of tapestries and waited. The shaft of light at the window dimmed and was gone. The Chamber was now in complete darkness, for the window was too far away to let in the flame of the torches in the courtyard.

The sound of chariot wheels brought Tirza to the window again. Toar was back from his fruitless search. He looked far from the self-confident young officer who had arrived to visit his grandmother earlier in the day, as he threw the reins to a stable-boy and hurried into the house.

Tirza waited until she was sure that Toar was in Gaava's room, then opened the door slightly.

"How dusty you look, my dear Toar," she heard her mistress exclaim. "And where have you been? And have you seen my pretty maiden?"

"Your pretty maiden is just the one I've been looking for," Toar cried. "Do you know that she is an

Israelite, placed here to spy on your son?"

"A spy, is she?" gasped Gaava in horror. "That little witch! I shall strangle her with my own hands!"

Toar laughed unpleasantly. "Let it not worry you, dear grandmother," he said. "She will trouble you no longer. If the guards do not find her, then the wild foxes will pick her bones white. Besides, we have the real plotters here in the dungeon." He paused for a moment. "Perhaps I should go down and have a word with them?"

Toar's hesitation was not lost on his grandmother. "Has your uncle asked you to speak with them?" she demanded.

"No, not exactly," Toar admitted. "Yet he did say that I should keep an eye on them."

Gaava laughed. "Have no worry, Toar. With Makke down there to guard them, they will surely remain where they are. He will flay them alive if they dare move a finger. Come my beloved Toar, we shall have the evening meal together, and you will talk to me of pleasant things. Now let me tell you about the finery from Ramah..."

Tirza closed the door. Gaava, she knew, did not usually retire for the night until some two hours after the evening meal, for she was a very hearty eater. With the excitement, however, she might want to prepare for bed earlier.

It was a good guess. Even before the meal had come to a close Gaava's eyelids began to droop, much to Toar's secret satisfaction. He was anxious to get away as quickly as possible and join his friends in the

123

tavern. He pretended to be disappointed when his grandmother bade him an early good night, but in another moment Tirza heard his footsteps hurrying down the corridor and out of the palace.

Tirza waited until all sound had died away, then left the Treasure Chamber and slipped quietly toward the stairway leading to the dungeon below. There was a heavy door at the head of the stairway, but Tirza knew that it was always left open to let the cool night air come in.

She crept down the stone steps and paused there. Makke's bed was across from the cells, on the other side of the iron post to which he bound his victims before whipping them. He was usually asleep at that hour, for it was his custom to rise in the middle of the night and walk about the iron post, flicking at it with his black whip. The slave girls who had been punished there were sure that Makke's purpose was to find new ways of tormenting them.

A taper was burning in the wall socket. In this light Tirza could see Makke's form, fully-clothed, sprawled on the low wooden bed. She moved on to the cells and peered through the rough opening gouged out in the door of each cell. The first was empty. In the second two figures were lying on the damp earthen floor.

"Heber!" Tirza called softly.

The figures on the floor stirred, then stiffened.

"Heber!" the girl repeated.

The Kenite's face was soon pressed to the hole in the door. "Is that you, Tirza?" he whispered. "How did you manage to escape Sisera's clutches?" He moved aside a little to let Nissan come close. "Have you learned anything?"

"I have," Tirza replied. "Sisera is going to demand of Jabin that he be given command of the foot soldiers too."

A groan came from Heber's lips. Nissan cursed softly. "When does Sisera intend to do this?" the Kenite asked.

"He may be on his way there now," Tirza answered. "He left the palace just before sunset." Her voice shook a little. "If Sisera succeeds, Heber, what will it mean to our cause?"

"Disaster — total disaster," returned Heber. "Sisera wants to weaken Prince Etzer's position in Hazor. And once he is in control of the foot soldiers, it will be impossible to draw him and his chariots into battle on Tabor."

Nissan cursed again. "Had it not been for that nephew of his, our plan could already have been working."

"You see," Heber explained to Tirza, "after the delivery of the horses to Sisera, I was going to tell him that we had seen Prince Etzer's troops moving south toward Tabor, and that the rumor was they were going to ring the mountain. This would deprive the charioteers of a chance for glory, and Sisera would certainly not stand by to see that happen."

"Then all is truly lost!" exclaimed Tirza in despair.

Heber shook his head. "Not yet. We do not *know* that Sisera's departure from the palace was for Hazor.

He has no reason to go there by night. And if he did not go to Hazor, one of us must get there first to warn Prince Etzer of Sisera's intention. The Prince could then be ready for him when he does get there." He drew a deep breath. "Can you get this door open, Tirza?" he asked.

"Makke has the key on a string around his neck," the girl replied. "But the loop is large. I will try to slip it off."

"No, no, you cannot take the risk," Heber began to protest.

Tirza was already at Makke's bedside. The cord was lying limp around the neck of the sleeping dungeon keeper. The girl gently eased her fingers under the cord, while her free hand grasped a small stool nearby. She swung the stool back and forth, then flung it against the iron pillar.

The noise was enough to disturb Makke's sleep. Still not completely awake, he raised his head, and in that instant the cord was gone.

"What is happening here, by Baal!" Makke growled. His eyes half-closed, he rose and lurched toward the cell, unaware of Tirza's presence halfway up the stairs. He peered through the window. The noise had not disturbed the two figures on the floor. Satisfied, the dungeon keeper turned around to head back for his bed when he caught sight of Tirza descending the steps.

"What is with you, Makke?" the girl exclaimed in feigned anger. "The sleep of my mistress is disturbed by the noise you are making. Beware, Makke, for she will have something to say to you."

Makke's face went pale. "W-what noise are you talking about?" he blurted. "E-verything is as quiet here as in a tomb."

"That is exactly where you may find yourself, Makke," Tirza retorted, "unless you go up and tell my mistress that the noise was not of your doing."

Makke blinked owlishly. His sleep-drugged mind was more and more confused.

"If the curtain across Gaava's chamber is open," continued Tirza, well knowing that it was not, "you are to enter and speak to her. If the curtain is closed, then you may come back here and I shall try to soothe her."

Makke's brain was clear enough to understand the difference. He hurried up the steps, hoping with all his pounding heart that the curtain was closed fast to the doorposts.

Heber and Nissan sprang to their feet. The next instant the door was open.

The Kenite embraced Tirza. "God should have blessed me with a daughter like you," he exclaimed. "That a mind so wise should dwell in one so young!" He turned to Nissan. "We must deal with the guard when he comes down without arousing the palace. Perhaps it is best that we let him fall asleep again and make our escape, even though there is not a moment to be lost."

Tirza raised a warning finger. "He is coming back!"

Heber and Nissan barely had time to lie down again behind the closed door when Makke came lum-

bering down, his bearded face wreathed in smiles.
"The noble Gaava is sleeping soundly. May Baal
shower blessings on her," he exclaimed. "Remember
now, tomorrow you put in a good word for me, hah ?"

Despite herself Tirza smiled at the vast relief in
Makke's voice. "I shall do that," she assured the dungeon keeper. "I shall tell my mistress that it was some
clumsy charioteer who disturbed her sleep."

As in echo of her words, the clutter of wheels
sounded in the courtyard. Tirza frowned, for this was
indeed strange. Sisera had forbidden the movement
of chariots at night in that area of the palace.

A gruff voice came through the open doorway. It
was Toar.

The young officer's face was flushed with the heavy
drinking he had done at the tavern. He had barely
managed to guide the chariot safely back to the palace, and now the lights of the tapers in the gates kept
dancing before his eyes, right at the spot where he
had warned his Uncle Sisera about the Israelite girl.

The memory of that scene angered Toar no end.
Why should his grandmother have forbidden him to
question the spies ?After all, it was he who had uncovered the plot, by Baal ; he and no one else ! And
if the girl had managed to get away for the moment,
the others had not ! If he, Toar, could make them
confess everything — yes, everything — he would be
a hero, indeed !

Toar crossed the threshold unsteadily and peered
into the gloom of the corridor until he located the
doorway at the head of the dungeon stairs. Down

below was Makke, torch in hand.

"Wake up the prisoners," ordered Toar thickly. "I want to question them."

Makke gulped. First Gaava with the noise, and now this one. Toar, Makke knew, was a favorite in the household, yet Sisera had ordered...

"What, stand you there, clod?" growled Toar. "Do as I say! Open the cell!" He drew his sword. "Open it, I say!"

"Yes, yes," Makke grunted in despair. His fingers fumbled for the cord around his neck. A wave of fear came over him as he found it gone.

"Well!" snapped Toar. "What is the matter, fool?"

"The cell key," groaned Makke. "It is gone!"

Toar raised his sword. "Then find it, by Baal," he cried, "or your head will find itself separated from your worthless body." He followed Makke across the dungeon chamber to his bed. Neither was aware of the girl huddling beneath the stone stairway.

The cell door creaked slightly, but before either Toar or Makke could straighten up from their search for the key, Heber and Nissan were upon them. Two well-aimed blows and the Canaanites, caught by surprise, fell limp on the bed.

"Hand us those ropes, Tirza," called Heber, pointing to the coils at the base of the pillar. These were the ropes with which Makke tied his victims to the iron post before whipping them. In another moment the men on the bed, gagged and trussed up like a pair of jackals, were dragged into the cell and locked there.

"And now what?" asked Nissan anxiously.

129

Heber led the way up the stairs. "You will get a horse, Nissan. The stable-boys are no doubt sound asleep. Ride to Hazor and make your way to Prince Etzer's palace. You may have to leave your horse outside the city, else the Canaanites will spot you. You will tell the Prince what Sisera has in mind. From there you will try to make for Tabor. By this time Barak should have up there most of the ten thousand men of Zevulun and Naftali."

"And you?" asked Nissan again.

The Kenite did not reply at once. Yes, what would he do? What *could* he do? "You will get a horse for Tirza, too, Nissan. And you, my brave girl, ride to Agnot and stay there with Ayal's wife. The place is near enough to Tabor yet out of range of the battle. I shall remain here."

Nissan shook his head. "That will be madness, Heber," he exclaimed. "You know what will happen if you are caught. Besides, what can you do?"

Heber faced Nissan squarely. "When there seems to be no hope, one must create it," he replied. "When Sisera returns, I must do something to drive him on to Tabor. Now go, both of you."

The three came out of the palace into the starlit night. No one was about. Beyond the gates, from the direction of the barracks, came muffled sounds, wisps of voices floating through the cool night air. Heber pointed wordlessly to the stables. His companions looked at him for a moment and then left him, hidden in the shadow of the palace wall.

At the stable Nissan made an unpleasant discovery.

There were three stable-men there, all asleep on the straw that littered the floor, but only one horse could be seen in the entire building.

"He will have to carry both of us," whispered Nissan.

"No, no," replied Tirza. "You will never get to Hazor that way. There is a clump of woods at the edge of the palace grounds. I can hide there, in a small cave that the slave girls showed me. They use it to hide from Makke until Gaava's temper calms down. I shall show you where it is, and you will come back for me when you can."

"What about food?" asked Nissan.

"The girls keep the cave well stocked, never fear," replied Tirza with a slight smile. "Now, go get the horse, and we shall find our way to the cave."

Nissan had a way with horses. The animal did not make a sound as Nissan led it out of the stable and around the edge of the courtyard to the clump of trees.

"The cave is over there," began Tirza, then froze in terror. Her finger was pointing straight at a dark hooded figure standing in the path. Nissan reached for his dagger.

"Come closer," came from the figure. Slowly the hood lifted.

Nissan gasped. "Yael!" he exclaimed. "In the name of the God of Deborah, what are you doing here?"

"I have come for my husband," the Kenite woman replied. "He is there in the shadows. Soon there will be tumult and fear — and death. I have come for him."

She reached out and grasped Tirza's hand. "You, girl, will be with me. You, other one, ride your horse, but only to Tabor. Clouds are gathering about Tabor. You must get there quickly. Go now, and falter not; disobey not."

Nissan glanced quickly at Tirza's white face. "I shall do so, Yael," he said. Without another word he tightened his grip on the reins and led his horse deeper into the woods. Suddenly he came to a halt. Off to one side, harnessed to a light cart, a mule was nibbling at the grass.

Nissan shivered and went on.

CHAPTER TEN

HEBER'S END

Sisera's destination was not Hazor.

The Canaanite commander had been turning Nehag's story over and over in his mind, and the more he thought about it, the less he was inclined to believe it. By the charioteer's own admission, the story had been brought to him by some servant in the household of Prince Etzer, and servants had a way of hearing things.

But more than that, Sisera felt, the whole story did not sound at all like the Prince, who was known to avoid quarrels as much as possible. Why, then, should he do something that would get him into deep trouble — and with the most powerful man in Canaan at that!

Instead of going to Hazor, Sisera turned off the main highway toward Rimmon. There, in a little village just before the town, lived the leather makers who supplied the thongs and harnesses for his horses. Sisera wanted a change in the width of the thongs, which he was sure would give the horses very much greater speed.

By the time that his visit had come to an end it was almost midnight, but Sisera refused the offer of the leather, makers to remain with them until morning. Heber and the girl he had brought with him kept preying on Sisera's mind, even though he knew his nephew Toar well enough to doubt his story, too. Still, Prince Etzer had said that the Kenite was "on good terms" with the royal court. Just what could that mean? Yes, Heber was an expert when it came to horses — but what more was he?

Sisera drove swiftly until he reached Haroshet-Hagoyyim. The sentinels at the gate jumped to their feet at the familiar sound of their commander's special chariot, but he drove past them straight to the palace entrance.

"Where are Toar and the girl?" he asked the sentry.

"Your nephew returned about an hour ago," was the reply, "but there was no girl with him."

"He said nothing to you?"

The sentry hesitated. "He said nothing," replied the sentry uneasily. "He... he did look a bit flushed — angry, I mean."

Sisera cursed under his breath. He had arranged the captaincy for Toar in the foot soldier battalion in order to keep track of Prince Etzer's plans, but Toar was interested in enjoying himself and little else. Well, Toar would have to be left for later, Sisera decided. There were the two prisoners to be questioned.

"Take your torch and come with me," he ordered the sentry.

A few paces from the palace a groan came from the shadow of the wall. Sisera stopped short, drew his sword from its sheath, and cautiously came closer.

The sentry raised his torch higher. On the ground, his face twisted as if in pain and clutching his leg, was Heber.

A cry of rage and surprise came from Sisera's lips. In two leaps he crossed the palace threshold and tore down the steps to the dungeon. The sentry, with one eye on the helpless man on the ground, edged closer to catch the strange sounds that came up through the open doorway.

Sisera was back in a moment, and his face was terrible to behold. "On your feet, Kenite," he thundered, smiting Heber on the back with the flat side of his sword.

"My leg! It is broken!" cried Heber. "They left me here, Baal curse them! May their flesh be eaten by dogs and may buzzards pick their bones! Oh, my leg!"

Sisera straightened up, as though hit by an unseen hand. "Speak, Kenite! Who freed you and the other one?"

"The curse of Baal be upon them!" wailed Heber. "May that Prince Etzer never see the sun rise again! Oh, my leg!"

Sisera went down to one knee and thrust his fist under Heber's chin. "Tell me who freed you," he said between gritted teeth, "or I shall hack you to pieces. Who was it?"

Heber drew a deep breath, as if to ease the pain.

"There were five of Etzer's men who came with us, to help us keep you occupied with horses and such."

"You lie!" roared Sisera. "Etzer would not dare send his men here!" He turned to the sentry. "In the dungeon you will find my dear nephew and Makke, both trussed up like geese. Cut their bonds loose and bring them here."

Heber, still clutching his leg, kept his half-closed eyes on Sisera's scowling face. The next few moments would tell the story.

Toar and Makke, still shaken by what had happened to them, staggered out of the palace. Sisera grasped each by his cloak, and drew them into the open. "Who attacked you?" he demanded.

Toar was trying desperately to collect his thoughts. He had no idea who had bound and gagged him, but he realized that he had to come up with a good tale. "There were at least five or six of them," he said thickly. "They came at us from behind, as we were looking in on the prisoners in the cell."

"You are sure that there were five or six?" Sisera cried.

"At least," ventured Makke eagerly. "Had there been three or four, we could have taken care of them easily." Like Toar, he was not anxious to have Sisera know that they had been caught unawares by the two prisoners. But how, in the name of Baal, did they get out?

Satisfied for the moment, Sisera again turned to Heber. "The whole story now," he snarled. "Every word, or the dogs will feed on your flesh."

The Kenite groaned. "Gladly will I tell you, O noble Sisera," he cried piteously. "I call unto Baal that your chariots get there in time to foil Prince Etzer — may the dust of the desert dry the marrow of his bones for having deserted me."

Sisera's eyes opened wide. Like a madman, he seized hold of Heber's drooping shoulders and shook him violently. "Speak quickly!" he shouted.

"Prince Etzer's troops left their encampment yesterday for Mount Tabor. I had brought him word that the Israelites were massing men there to cut off the main highway. The Prince will surround the mountain and starve the Israelites into surrender. This will show all Canaan that victory can be gained without your chariots. Oh, my leg!"

Sisera let out a bellow of rage that rang like a thunder clap through the palace grounds. Sentries and charioteers came running to the scene. They stood there, gasping in amazement. Their commander's face was purple with rage. His eyes, in the flickering flames of the torches, bulged from his brow like burning coals. His arms shook, as he fought to keep himself under control. Heber could feel the heat of Sisera's rage towering above him.

"And all this time you were selling me horses, scoundrel!"

"May Baal forgive me," moaned Heber. "The Prince ordered me to keep you here as long as possible, so that your chariots might not get to Tabor before his soldiers." He pointed a trembling finger at Toar. "That is why your nephew was given leave, so that he would not know all this and come to warn you."

Sisera barely glanced at the open-mouthed Toar. "What did the noble Prince Etzer promise you for your work, Kenite?"

"Twenty sheep and thirty pieces of silver," groaned Heber.

"Here is what I shall give you!" roared Sisera. He swung up his heavily-sandaled foot. It caught Heber on the temple, knocking him flat on the ground. As the Kenite lay there stunned, his eyes glazing, Sisera brought his foot down on Heber's bare head with all his weight. There was a sickening sound as Heber's skull shattered under the savage blow.

"Throw him into the woods," shouted Sisera to the silent sentries. "Have the bugler call every charioteer out into the parade ground." Without another word he turned and stalked into the palace, breathing heavily through foam-flecked lips.

He found Gaava on her couch, shaking with fear. She half rose, then fell back again, covering her tearful face.

"Etzer has finally challenged me," Sisera cried. "But be not afraid, my mother. This time I shall crush him. His soldiers need two days to get to Tabor from their camp. I shall be there with my chariots before noon tomorrow."

Gaava did not understand one word of what her son was saying, but she knew that he was not happy and again she burst into tears.

Sisera felt his patience wearing thin, but he loved his mother too much to hurt her feelings. "No more

crying, please," he said. "Remember, when I am done with Etzer, all the finery of his household will be yours. I shall see to that. I promise you."

The thought of owning Princess Piria's finery was very pleasant to Gaava. Her tears ceased flowing like magic and a smile wreathed her round face. Sisera, greatly relieved, bade his mother goodbye and left the palace.

The grounds in front of the charioteers' barracks were now ablaze with the glow of a hundred torches. When Sisera arrived he found every one of his men, charioteers and warriors alike, waiting for him. •

The Canaanite commander mounted a flat stone at one end of the square enclosure. "Fighting men of Canaan, my own warriors," he began, his voice piercing the still night air, "you are to prepare at once to leave for Mount Tabor on whose heights a pack of Israelite jackals has gathered to bay revolt against Canaan. Your captains will lead you in a charge up the slope for about two hundred paces. You will leave your chariots there and go on to press the Israelites up the mountain to the very top. There you will deal death to every man you find, and the whole land will ring with praises of your noble deeds. And death to anyone — *anyone,* I repeat, who tries to stop your ascent up Tabor!"

A loud cheer broke from the ranks of the charioteers crowded in front of their commander. If anyone had any question about the wisdom of charging up Tabor, none was there to voice it.

"Prepare your armor and chariots," continued Sisera, "and rein up in full array at the gates!"

By this time, the whole town was awake. The towns-people, feeling that something unusual was afoot, gathered about the barracks and crowded near the main gate leading out to the highway. It did not take long for all sorts of rumors to begin flying about their expeditions. Thus it was that, at one and the same time, the townspeople swore that the chariots were on their way to enslave the Ammonites, seize the wealth of Gilead, and cleave their way through Philistia for the conquest of Egypt itself.

Dawn was still an hour away when Sisera, with his armor bearer crouching behind him in the large chariot, drove through the ranks of chariots at the gate and took his place at their head. He turned around for a last look at the host behind him. This was his pride and power, this array of nine hundred chariots. Never in history had there been so powerful a fighting, smashing force! Sisera's heart swelled. Hah! Had he only lived in the days when the Israelite upstarts crossed the Jordan into Canaan! His chariots would have trampled down the invaders like helpless weeds in the field.

The only one in the entire host who did not share the high spirits of the Canaanite commander was Nehag. Thick-witted most of the time, his mind had been set into confused motion at the mention of Mount Tabor. There was something strange about the whole matter. The scene of Arnon telling his story of the plot kept passing through Nehag's head, even as he kept his chariot in line with all the other chariots along the highway.

Quiet now descended once more on Haroshet-Ha-goyyim, although many a townsman lay awake wondering whether the chariots were on their way to Ammon, Gilead, or Egypt. In Baal's name, they could not be heading for all three at the same time! But then, Sisera was always victorious; why worry?

Silence reigned, too, in the palace grounds. Gaava was fast asleep. In the room next to hers was Toar. Not being a charioteer, he had orders from his uncle to remain behind and keep watch. This did not please Toar at all, but his displeasure disappeared along with the contents of the jug that lay on the soft rug beside him.

On his cot in the dungeon Makke slept with a snoring and wheezing which did not disturb the entire palace only because the heavy door at the head of the stairs was shut tight. The dungeon keeper had given up trying to guess what had happened, and he certainly had no desire to think about what Sisera might yet decide to do with him.

And just inside the woods, only a moist patch of ground marked the spot where Sisera's servants had cast Heber's body. But the body itself was no longer there. Nor had anyone heard, amid the rattle of the chariots, the sound of cartwheels rolling along the grassy turf toward one of the smaller gates leading out of the town.

The two women on the wooden driver's seat spoke not a word. Tirza was still fighting off the shock that had seized her when she saw Sisera's foot come down on Heber's head. As in a nightmare she had watched the Kenite's body being dragged from where it lay to the edge of the woods, not thirty paces away from the clump of bushes behind which she and Yael were hiding. Then came those hideous moments of pain-filled waiting... waiting... waiting until no one was about, while all that time Yael stood motionless, her eyes fixed on the crumpled form of her husband.

Now Heber's broken body was lying under the straw matting in the cart, and Yael was taking him... where? Tirza's brain was still in a whirl. If Yael knew what was going to happen, why had she allowed her husband to go to Haroshet-Hagoyyim? Then, as the pain slowly began to lift, Tirza understood. Heber had a mission to fulfill, a mission greater than the value of one human life — even the life of a beloved husband! Tirza had a strong desire to embrace the woman beside her, to weep with her.

But Yael was not crying. As the first streaks of dawn broke through the darkness to the east, the Kenite woman broke the silence.

"We shall reach the home of Ayal at sunrise," she said in her strange, low voice. "I shall leave you there with those who will care for you."

Ayal? Heber had mentioned Ayal...

"And what will you do?" asked Tirza gently.

"I shall take Heber to his resting place. It will be by the banks of the stream, near our tent. Then I shall fold my tent, take my belongings and place them in this cart."

"You will go back to your people?"

143

"No, my daughter. There is none of my family left in the south."

"Where will you go ? I know that my people..."

Yael held up her hand for silence. "Thank you, my daughter. But I must go pitch my tent by the side of the road from Mount Tabor to the north."

"But you will be caught in the battle !"

"I shall pitch my tent there and wait for him."

"Wait for him ? For whom ?"

"For my husband's murderer."

CHAPTER ELEVEN

THUNDER OVER TABOR

It was only when Sisera's scouts reported Prince Etzer's troops were not yet in the area that the Canaanite commander ordered a halt for the morning meal, an hour's distance from Tabor.

This was the opportunity for which Nehag had been waiting ever since the chariot army left Haroshet-Hagoyyim. He simply had to speak to Sisera.

Driving in the brisk night air of northern Canaan, Prince Etzer's banished charioteer had kept thinking of that evening in the stable when Arnon had first hinted at the plans for the Israelite revolt. No one had believed the story then, yet here was Sisera, who had ridiculed the rumor more strongly than anyone else — yes, here was Sisera himself, at the head of all the chariots, heading for Tabor! Something was wrong, very wrong!

Nehag finished his meal quickly and made his way to the vanguard of the chariot cavalcade, where Sisera was holding council with his captains. The charioteer waited at a respectful distance until the group of leaders disbanded.

Sisera caught sight of Nehag and grunted with displeasure. Nehag reminded him of Prince Etzer, an unwelcome presence at any time. "What is it?" he rasped.

"A word with you, Commander," the charioteer asked.

"Speak your word."

Nehag squirmed, not at all sure of himself. "It is about that Israelite youth," he began, "the one who first told us about the revolt, back in Prince... in Hazor. I think... that is, do you think...?"

"Speak," growled Sisera impatiently, "or go back to your chariot. What is it?"

"I... I think it is some kind of trap, O Sisera," stammered Nehag. "I have felt it all along, felt it in my veins." He plodded on. "Ever since we left Hazor, sir, I felt it, sir, in my veins."

Sisera gave the charioteer a baleful glare. "Your veins are the veins of a fool," he declared, "and your brains are no wiser than your veins. Return to your chariot and let not your tongue flap about so loosely. Go!"

Nehag slunk away like a whipped cur, but now his mind was made up. Let Sisera and all the others go ahead and attack Mount Tabor: at the first sign of trouble he, Nehag, would turn his chariot around and drive away. A man's mind might deceive him, yes, but *not* his veins, by Baal!

There was not the slightest hint of trouble, however, as the chariots drew within sight of the lofty

146

mountain. Overhead the bright morning sun shone clear and the sky stretched in all directions like a blue dome; the plain below lay quiet and serene in the sunshine. Beyond Tabor, etched with the tufts of grass that marked it's course, was the Kishon river bank.

Sisera's lips curled in triumph. By the time Prince Etzer's troops reached the scene, the Israelites — if they were indeed atop Tabor — would be routed and their revolt crushed. Sisera chuckled to himself as he imagined the surprised look on Prince Etzer's face when he discovered that his prize had been snatched away from him. Ah, yes! There would also be a little score to settle about that Kenite spy. It was fortunate indeed, by Baal, that the fool had broken his leg and could not get away with the others, else Prince Etzer's scheme would not have been exposed. Yes, the fate of the Kenite would surely teach Prince Etzer a lesson!

Five hundred paces from the foot of Tabor, with the foot soldiers still nowhere in sight, Sisera signaled for a halt. He could not detect the slightest movement on the slopes of the mountain, but the Israelites were there, he was sure.

Again the Canaanite commander waved his hand around his head. At this, the array of chariots split smartly to the left and to the right in full encirclement of the mountain. To Barak and his men, perched high on the slopes, the chariots below looked like a swarm of well-trained ants.

The Israelite commander had spent a sleepless night.

Not until Nissan came, an hour before dawn, did Barak have any idea when Sisera would strike.

Nissan himself could tell very little. He had briefly informed Barak of how he and Heber had been caught by Toar's appearance and imprisoned, and how Tirza had freed them. He told how Heber had insisted on remaining behind. But why Yael was there and with a cart — this Nissan could not explain. Neither could Barak. In his heart he knew that Heber would not give up until his mission had been fulfilled. Now Sisera and his chariots were at Tabor, but what had been Heber's fate?

Barak pushed his thoughts aside and leaned farther out on the flat rock from which he had been watching the movements of the charioteers. The encircling movement was now complete. Was Sisera's intention to besiege the mountain and no more? Barak strained his eyes, looking for something that would give him the answer. No, if only a siege had been ordered by Sisera, the charioteers would not remain standing in their chariots.

The blast of a bugle came up from the valley below. At the signal, the chariots began to move. With gathering speed they converged on the mountain in a cloud of dust that hid the sun.

Suddenly, unseen by the charioteers in the dust of their own chariots, Tabor was overcast with dark clouds, and a wild wind began whipping through the trees. As the massed Israelites on the mountain top threw themselves to the ground to escape the force of the wind, a torrent of rain broke in blinding sheets like a flood, amid stabs of lightning and peals of crashing thunder. Stones and chunks of earth were uprooted as by a giant hand, and the rushing waters washed them down the mountainside straight at the oncoming chariots.

At the first crash of thunder, the horses pulling the chariots broke their stride and reared back, ignoring the frantic whiplashes of the charioteers. The captains tried to rally their squads and halt the stampede, but in vain. The horses, ankle deep in the torrent, were now out of control. Overturned chariots and horses rolled down the mountainside in a mass of horror; they were carried down to the Kishon, where the swollen current swept them off in twisted clumps of wreckage.

Sisera had abandoned his chariot at the beginning of the rout. He started up the slope on foot to help his captains bring their charioteers under control, but one look was enough to show him that the situation was hopeless. Quickly he loosed his armor and flung it to the ground, keeping only his sword and helmet. Bending low, he made his way unrecognized between the rocking chariots toward the bottom of the mountain. A few more steps and he would have been clear of his shuttered army, when suddenly he felt something clamp itself like a vise around his ankle. As he struggled to break away, he looked down to see what had trapped him.

It was Nehag. Pinned down by his own overturned chariot, his leg badly crushed, the charioteer had recognized the face and build of his commander just as the latter was about to pass by.

"Ah, the brave leader is deserting his men," Nehag croaked, holding on savagely to Sisera's ankle. "I warned you, Sisera! I told you I felt it in my veins that there was trouble ahead. Now you shall not get away! You will die with me and all the others!"

Sisera wasted no time. He swiftly drew his sword and, in a single motion, brought it down upon the helpless charioteer, severing his arm at the shoulder. Nehag gave one shriek, and Sisera was free. He leaped over the charioteer's writhing body, stumbled in the mud, and staggered on.

Then, just as suddenly as it had come, the rain stopped. The clouds vanished and the sun shone brightly on the remnants of the Canaanite forces in full flight and pursued by the Israelites. No one seemed to notice the solitary figure running in quite another direction, as though some unseen force was drawing him on to the north.

Shortly after dawn on the day of the battle, one of Ayal's maidservants went out to the courtyard to draw water from the well. She was about to lower the bucket when she saw a crumpled figure lying on the ground by the gate.

The frightened girl ran back for help. At the entrance to the farmhouse she found Arnon, propped up against the wall, dozing fitfully.

Like everyone else at Ayal's, whither he had been sent by Barak to serve as a courier for the Prophetess, Arnon was anxiously awaiting the events of the coming days. Yet with all the excitement around him, the boy found himself thinking about Prince Etzer. The Canaanite nobleman, he felt sure, would not break the promise he had made to Barak. No, he would not order his men to Tabor — at least not until Sisera and his chariots had made the first move.

What then ? Even if Sisera were to meet with defeat, Prince Etzer would still have to proceed against the Israelites. All of Canaan would demand that he do this at once, and the Prince himself was not one to ignore a challenge.

Then, a few hours before Ayal's maidservant aroused him, Arnon was called to the room that the Prophetess was occupying in the farmhouse. One of the Israelite scouts had just returned from Hazor with a report which Deborah wanted the youth to hear.

Prince Etzer, the scout reported, had returned to the palace from some mysterious overnight trip. In the morning he awoke with a strange pain in his head. He could neither speak nor hear. The court physician was summoned but no cure could be found. Princess Piria then ordered the family carriage to be made ready. The servants placed the Prince in the carriage. With the Princess and young Nasik by his side, Prince Etzer was escorted from Hazor to Tyre, on the Phoenician coast, where he would be attended by the physicians of Tyre, said to be the foremost masters in the art of healing.

The report saddened Arnon deeply, yet it also set his mind at ease ; if Sisera were defeated, no other threat would face the Israelites. Still he could not forget Prince Etzer's kindness toward him. He was half-dreaming about young Nasik in the runaway chariot when the maidservant shook him out of his nap.

"Something strange, by the gate," she whispered hoarsely. "Come!"

Arnon got to his feet quickly and followed the woman. From a distance he could not tell what the heap on the ground could be. As he came near, he reached down and turned the strange figure so that the gray morning light was upon it.

His heart almost stopped beating. It was Tirza.

"Go get some help," Arnon ordered the servant girl. He threw back the hood from Tirza's head. A slight moan came from the girl's parted lips and her eyes fluttered open. But although they looked straight at Arnon there was not the slightest sign of recognition in them. He loosened the cloak about her neck, hardly aware that his fingers had grown clumsy, numb with his fear for her.

The maidservant returned with several others. One of them carried a thick straw mat. They placed Tirza on the mat and bore her to the farmhouse. Deborah, summoned from her brief sleep, met the group at the doorway. "Place her in my bed," she directed.

To Arnon it seemed that hours passed before the Prophetess showed herself again. "Tirza is hot with fever," she announced, "but she will be well."

Just then a strange rumbling sound brought Arnon, weak with relief, out of the house and to the south fence. Far away across the plain, speeding toward Tabor, was the host of Sisera's chariots, half-hidden in the swirl of yellow dust. Moments passed, then came the ring around the mountain. Someone near Arnon pointed to the sky. There it was as Yael had foretold — the sudden massing of clouds over Tabor, the mighty cloudburst, the blinding flashes, the claps of strident thunder. Arnon's heart beat with excitement. The very heavens were fighting on the side of his people!

He looked back toward the house. The Prophetess was standing in the doorway, tall and majestic in her long white cloak. With arms upraised and eyes closed she stood there, until suddenly all sound ceased and the sun shone forth again over the mountain.

Now there was nothing to do but await word from Barak himself.

It came a scant hour later. Nissan arrived, riding a lathered horse which he had managed to unhitch from one of the chariots. Sisera's forces had been completely routed. The few who had escaped the flood of rain and rock were now in full flight along the same highway which had witnessed the thunderous advance of the Canaanites only hours earlier.

"Come with me," said Deborah.

She led Nissan to the chamber where Tirza was still shaking with fever. At the sight of Nissan, the girl tried to get up.

"You did not see him," she cried, flinging out her arms. "He was on the ground, and Sisera's foot came down on his head... Yael, where are you taking me?... Like the shell of an egg... I covered him with straw, Yael, but the cart is shaking it off..."

She fell back on the bed.

Nissan looked from Tirza to the Prophetess. "Heber?" he asked, his lips trembling.

Deborah nodded and from her eyes the tears flowed freely. "We found her by the gate. Yael must have brought her as far as Ayal's and then gone on."

Nissan clenched his fists. "Barak will catch up with Sisera if he has to pursue him as far as Phoenicia. And when he does..."

"No, no!" Again Tirza tried to sit upright, and this time the fever seemed almost to have gone from her voice. "Sisera is not there! Yael is waiting for him in her tent by the side of the road. She is there, waiting for him!"

"Yael is indeed waiting for Sisera," the Prophetess said quietly. "Nissan and Arnon, take your horses and ride to Haroshet-Hagoyyim. When you overtake Barak, tell him to come back to Tabor. He will see the tent... and Sisera."

From the foot of Mount Tabor a trail ran northward. It was little used by travelers because its course lay through a thick stand of timber which allowed hardly any passage for vehicles or even pack-animals. Only young folk on camping trips took this trail to get to the mountain, and many a tree bore the carved names of those who had passed that way.

This was the trail that Sisera took, fleeing blindly from the scene of his defeat. By the time the Canaanite commander reached the woods, the sounds of battle had dwindled to the distant cries of the routed charioteers. He took off his helmet and wiped the sweat from his eyes. A low limb of a nearby tree beckoned to him; Sisera leaned across the limb, letting his body droop over it in utter weariness. His mind was in a haze. What could have happened to his mighty host, his invincible chariots? A rainstorm, and at this time of the year? What was it that Nehag had said?

Sisera raised his head and looked about him. He needed a place to hide. The Israelites would, of course, search for his body amid the wreckage on Tabor. Not finding it, they would scour the country-side. Where could he hide? Not in these woods; this would be the first place they would search.

He straightened up and staggered on along the twisting trail. Once beyond the woods, he might chance upon a farmer and his cart. The helmet would give him away; he tossed it into the bushes. There was his sword. Sisera hesitated, then threw it away as well. Now he was not Sisera, the terror of Canaan's enemies, but a footsore traveler.

At the edge of the woods he stopped short. Some twenty paces farther, just to the right of the trail, stood a tent. At its top, woven into the black fabric, was a brown stripe, symbol of the Kenites.

Sisera's eyes brightened. There was peace between King Jabin and the Kenites.

The scene of Heber in the courtyard of the palace flashed through his mind, but Sisera pushed it away. Whoever lived in the tent could not know what had happened in Haroshet-Hagoyyim less than a day earlier!

As if in echo to Sisera's thought, the tent flap moved aside and a woman came out. She stood there, her dark face drawn in a smile of welcome, and beckoned to the Canaanite commander. "Come, my dear sir," she called out in a husky, warm voice. "Come to me, and be not afraid."

A crafty smile came to Sisera's dust-caked lips. By Baal, what could be better? The Israelites would not think of searching a woman's tent! And this woman seemed to be so friendly.

He bent down and half-stumbled into the tent. It was cool inside, and dark. Soft goatskins covered the earthen floor. Sisera sank to the ground.

"A little water," he pleaded. "I am so thirsty."

Sisera sensed rather than saw Yael moving about in the tent. Then she was kneeling beside him, a deep earthen dish in her hands. "I have milk for you," she whispered. "It is fresh from the goatskin. It is much better than water. It will put you to sleep quickly, and you will rest."

Sisera struggled to one elbow and pressed his parched lips to the bowl. He gulped the milk down in two, three deep drafts. "Much better than water," he mumbled. He raised himself higher. "I want you to stand at the entrance to the tent," he said to Yael. "Should anyone ask you: 'Is there any man inside?' you will answer: 'There is none,' you understand?"

"I understand," replied Yael. "I understand very well. I swear, by your life and as long as you live, that no one shall cross the threshold."

Sisera lowered himself to the skins. Something fluffy

156

hovered above him and covered his body. Ah, this wonderful woman was spreading a soft blanket over his tired frame! What good fortune! Yes, a few hours of slumber and he would arise a new man. There were some scores to settle. Prince Etzer! Yes, a few scores...

The sound of deep breathing now filled the tent. It grew louder, then settled into a gentle snore. A gust of wind came through the flap. It caught a corner of the wool blanket and curled it back, revealing the hairy temple of the sleeping man.

Yael now threw back the hood that covered her head, and her raven black hair came tumbling down her thin shoulders. In her eyes a deep light began to burn, like a candle in the blackness of a cave. She knelt by the sleeping Canaanite and bent low, so that her lips were but a hand's breadth away from the uncovered temple.

"Hear me, O Commander Sisera," she whispered. "Hear the words of Yael, wife of Heber the Kenite, the man whose life you snuffed out, whose crushed body you ordered thrown to the dogs, to whose tent you have come for shelter from your pursuers — you, the mighty Sisera, routed in battle, your glory ground to dust. Listen to me now, for my words will be the last that your ears will ever hear. Yes, you asked for water; I gave you milk. It was a large dish in which I brought the milk to you, was it not? Heber's dish it was, and from it he slaked his thirst, in the comfort of this tent. From it you have had your last gulp, just as in your courtyard Heber drew his last breath. You have asked me to keep your pursuers away; by your life and as long as you live I have promised to obey, for by the time they who seek you reach this tent, you will not be among the living, O Sisera! Yes, you, the hero of Canaan, before whom all tremble, you will die — and at the hands of a woman, a lowly woman in a Kenite tent."

A chilling gust of wind came through the flap. Sisera, under the warm blanket, did not stir.

Yael arose. From a small chest she brought forth a long wooden tent peg. Its sharp point gleamed white in the half light. In the chest also lay an adze-like hammer, sharp and wide-edged on one side, rounded and blunt on the other, like a mallet.

Yael's fingers tightened around the wooden handle. Peg and hammer in her hands, she kneeled again by Sisera's sleeping body, by the uncovered temple. Her face as calm as the sea on a summer day, Yael raised the tent peg and held it firmly above Sisera's temple, its white point almost resting on the matted black hair. Slowly she raised the hammer. Still Sisera slept.

Now a swirl of sand came blowing into the tent, into Sisera's nostrils. He lay quietly, calmly, for he was dead. Through his temple, its point no longer white, was the tent peg driven so hard that it pierced Sisera's head and drove into the ground beneath it, pounded home by the hand of a woman.

Almost within sight of Haroshet-Hagoyyim the road cut through between two steep embankments which controlled the approach to the town.

Here the last surviving charioteers planned to make a stand against the pursuing Israelites. Only a few chariots had escaped the disaster at Tabor, and one of these was sent ahead to Haroshet-Hagoyyim to bring help. But it was too late. A score of Barak's men, riding hard to this spot, had rolled down a heap of boulders from the embankments to the road beneath, making it impassable.

In vain did the townspeople of Haroshet-Hagoyyim wait for Sisera and his invincible chariots to return. Not one of the remaining charioteers was left to tell the story.

Barak summoned his captains. No report had been received that Sisera was either dead or a captive, although every piece of wreckage had been carefully searched. The Canaanite commander seemed to have vanished into thin air. Perhaps he was still on Tabor, the captains suggested. Barak shook his head; no one could have made his way *up* the mountain against the torrent of rain and mud.

The Israelite leader was considering an advance on Haroshet-Hagoyyim itself when Nissan and Arnon arrived. Barak listened to their account and ordered his men back to Tabor. It was almost evening when they neared the mountain, moving along in a wide fanned-out arc to take in all the approaches to the scene of the battle. As they neared the wood, Barak signaled for a halt. Like a monument set in a lonely field, the tent of Heber the Kenite stood silent in the falling darkness.

Barak went on alone, his heart heavy with grief and

fear. What could he say to Yael, whose husband had given his life for the Israelite cause? And if Sisera was in the tent, would Yael be alive?

The tent flap moved aside just as Barak drew near, and Yael came out. "Come," she said simply, "and I will show you the man whom you are seeking."

She stepped aside to let Barak pass. He went in, and the Kenite woman held back the flap to let the feeble light come through. On the soft skins, the tent peg through his head and imbedded in the earth under it, lay Sisera, the mighty warrior, the strong man of Canaan, dead at the hands of a woman.

Barak led Yael out of the tent. Overhead the stars were coming out one by one, until the entire sky was twinkling with their pinpoints of light. A soft breeze came through the wood, the branches moving as with the sound of a lullaby.

"Heber was our best friend," said Barak, "a man whose heart could not bear to see anyone chained by tyranny. He loved this land, too, all of it, and he hated anyone who defiled it by oppressing anyone else who called this land his home. We loved him because to us, too, this land is sacred. It is now hallowed even more because his blood is part of its soil. There it will always be, to bring its message of friendship and courage to all who seek freedom."

A LETTER FROM ARNON, SON OF BARAK,
TO HIS SON YA'IR

My dear son,

Word has reached us that you are now preparing your caravans for the long journey to Egypt, through the territory of Judah and the Negev. May the God of our fathers lend blessing to the work of your hands, so that you and your family will prosper.

You may have occasion in the course of your travels to pass through Ophra, in the territory of Manasseh. If you do, stop at the home of Joash, the head of the Aviezer clan, and inquire about his health, for he is a friend of mine. Of late his tribe had been oppressed by the Midianites and the Amalekites. This grieves me but it comes as no surprise for, as I have often told my friend Joash, the tribes of Israel still have to learn what we of Naftali learned fifty years ago: if we take unto ourselves the ways of our neighbors, they will turn on us.

I have told you the story of our own strife with the kingdom of Hazor. Your mother, Tirza, cradled you to sleep with the songs of our people's victory over Sisera. Perhaps if our brethren of Manasseh had seen the deeds of the Lord in those days, as we did, they would not abandon Him so readily now.

In Egypt, my son, you will see other peoples; you will hear of other gods. They have not changed much since the liberation of our people under Moses more than two hundred years ago. Bear this in mind: that you are descended from the people who crossed the Sea of Reeds when the Lord turned it dry for them. Some day we shall cease being tribes and become a nation, as on the day when our fathers stood at Sinai.

Therefore I am writing this letter to you, my son. I want to fill your heart with that which your parents felt when, together with many thousands of Israel, they came to Ramah to thank the Lord for the victory over Sisera. This took place fully six years before your mother and I were joined in marriage. I hope that my words will give eyes to your mind, so that you, too, will picture the day as we did, and remember it.

Even though only Sisera's chariots had been destroyed and the Canaanite army was yet to be reckoned with, we at Ramah were not dismayed. We knew that every heart in Hazor would melt at the news of what had taken place on Mount Tabor, just as did the hearts of all in Canaan when Joshua led our people through the parted waters of the Jordan.

Ramah was overflowing with people, many more than on the day I first saw it for the Spring Market many years ago. All of us were eager to hear the

163

Prophetess proclaim, in her own words, the story of our triumph. Your grandfather, Barak, was to stand by her side.

The proclamation became known as "the Song of Deborah." I caught sight of many scribes writing the words down on their scrolls as the Prophetess uttered them. Nimble of fingers they were, those scribes; before the day was over, hundreds of scrolls were being sold at wondrous prices. You know, of course, that the scroll we have in our possession is the one written by the Prophetess herself, which she gave to us as her gift on our wedding day. When you were a young lad, you knew every word on that scroll by heart. Lest you have forgotten, I shall note a few of the verses here.

Deborah began her song by asking the people to praise the Lord because it was He who had given them the will, after years of enslavement, to strike a blow for their freedom. Then she said:

> Hear, O kings! Lend ear, O princes!
> To the Lord now I shall sing,
> I shall give song to the Lord God of Israel.

We still remembered the crashing storm which had struck Sisera on Tabor, but Deborah's next words, describing the gathering of our ancestors at Mount Sinai, reminded us even more of the miracle we had witnessed with our own eyes:

> O Lord, when you came forth from Se'ir,
> When you went on from Edom's field,
> The earth shook, the heavens dripped,
> Yes, the massed clouds dripped water.

Mountains melted away before the Lord,
Even Sinai — before the Lord, God of Israel.

The tribes of Naftali and Zevulun, Deborah reminded us, were not the first to suffer oppression, nor was Jabin the first to place the yoke of bondage upon the neck of our people. Many years before Sisera's appearance in Hazor, our people had tasted slavery — not as did our forefathers in Egypt, to be sure, but they did not have the freedom of a people living on its own soil. Yes, the Lord promised this land to us, yet many peoples and tribes living here at the time of Joshua were not conquered by him, so that each coming generation would have to gain a bit of freedom all by itself and not as a gift from the past. There are still the Philistines and the Sidonites, and besides them the old enemies of our people on the other side of the Jordan. Moab, Midian, Ammon and Amalek have not forgotten their defeat at the hands of Moses.

To save our people from their enemies, the Lord sent men of courage at the hour of danger: Ehud, the left-handed one, and Shamgar, the son of Anat. Still the land was not safe. We had to avoid the highways and travel over hidden trails. The small towns were abandoned. The fortified cities were filled with fear. We were without a leader.... unitl Deborah came, a true mother for our people, and brought hope for freedom to our hearts. From other tribes help came to us in our revolt against Hazor. Among the ten thousand on Mount Tabor on that great day were men of Ephraim, Benjamin, Manasseh and Issachar. But there were others who did not come, and Deborah

165

did not spare them:

> *By the watercourses of Reuben there were*
> *Mighty deliberations. Why did you retire*
> *To the sheepfold and listen to the*
> *Piping of the shepherds of the flocks?*
> *Indeed, weighty were the deliberations*
> *By the watercourses of Reuben!*

How my heart was pained when I heard these simple words! They brought to my mind Heber, the noble Kenite, and the sacrifice that he made for our freedom. How disheartened he was when he returned from his fruitless mission to the Reubenites! I remember how ashamed we felt when he came back with the tidings — to think that our people, our flesh and blood, were unwilling to come to our aid, while here was the son of another people... I find it difficult to write about Heber, even after all these years...

Still, we won the battle. Had we lost it, there on the banks of the Kishon, we would have fallen prey to every Canaanite chieftain in the land. But rest assured, my son, that it was the manner in which Sisera was defeated that struck fear into their hearts:

> *From the heavens they were given battle;*
> *The stars in their courses fought Sisera:*
> *The Kishon, that ancient stream, swept them away.*
> *Take strength from this, O my soul!*

So recited Deborah, and for a moment we thought that her song was at an end, that we would all be going to our homes, grateful to the woman into whose hands the Lord had delivered Sisera. But we were wrong:

166

Of all women let Yael be the most blessed,
She the wife of Heber the Kenite,
Of all women may she be blessed in her tent.
He asked for water; she handed him milk,
The richest of milk in a generous dish.
Then her hand she stretched forth to the tent peg,
And her right hand reached toward the hammer.
She smote Sisera, crushed his head,
Split his temple from side to side.
At her feet he lay, fallen, stricken,
Dead on the spot he had first lain down.

All about me I read astonishment on every face.
Yael the Kenite? Why should she have killed Sisera,
the Commander of friendly Canaan — and in so fierce
a fashion? Yet you must remember that only a hand-
ful of us knew how Heber had met his death. Therefore did Deborah call Yael the "wife" of Heber and
not his widow. Ah, Yael, Yael! She was never seen
again after we removed Sisera's body from her tent.
She did not even tell us where she had buried Heber,
her husband, our friend.

And now the song was indeed approaching its close.
Knowing how bitter our people had become over the
heavy burdens that Jabin had placed upon them,
Deborah went on:

Through the window
(how well your mother remembers it!)
Sisera's mother whimpered... Why is his chariot force
So late? Why do the wheels of his chariot tarry?
Her witty friends find replies, and she too
Finds ready answers for herself: It must be that

They have come upon much booty to be divided ...
Thus may all your foes, O Lord, now perish;
But as for those who love the Lord, may they
Be as the sun going forth in its might.

This, O my son, your mother and I want you to remember. If you love the Lord, if you know in your heart that he is the source of your strength, then indeed you will be as the sun, mighty in your own course and giving light and warmth to others, who will love you in turn. Remember this as you go on your journeys, and keep it in your heart. It took us years of hardship and an awesome battle to learn this. I bid you take this lesson to heart.

Your father,
Arnon, son of Barak.